D0433250

MY WHOLE WORLD JUMPED

My Whole World Jumped

Jonathan Brant

KINGSWAY PUBLICATIONS
EASTBOURNE

Copyright © Jonathan Brant 2002

The right of Jonathan Brant to be identified
as the author of this work has been asserted by him in
accordance with the Copyright, Designs
and Patents Act 1988.

First published 2002

All rights reserved.
No part of this publication may be reproduced or
transmitted in any form or by any means, electronic
or mechanical, including photocopy, recording or any
information storage and retrieval system, without
permission in writing from the publisher.

Unless otherwise indicated, biblical quotations are
from the New International Version © 1973, 1978, 1984
by the International Bible Society.

ISBN 0 85476 765 7

Published by
KINGSWAY COMMUNICATIONS LTD
Lottbridge Drove, Eastbourne, BN23 6NT, England.
Email: books@kingsway.co.uk

Book design and production for the publishers by
Bookprint Creative Services, P.O. Box 827, BN21 3YJ, England.
Printed in Great Britain.

Dedication

To Tricia and to Isaac, naturally.

And to the young people of the Parish of Holy Trinity Brompton with St Paul's Onslow Square, and of the Iglesia Anglicana del Uruguay.

Thanks

This book is the result of much hard work, only a fraction of it mine.

I would like to thank Jo Glen, Richard Herkes and James Heard for great editorial support; Nicky Gumbel for setting me loose to adapt *Questions of Life* in such a radical way; and the many young people (and adults) who read and commented on the manuscripts:

Jacob Baratta; the Brooks boys (Ben and Jonathan); Luke Carter; George Costa; Kate Godfree; Zilla, Alice, Hannah, Martha, Tilly, Will and Rupert Hawkins; Eleanor Herkes; Pippa, Henry, Johnny and Rebekah Gumbel; Fi Millar; Andrew Neill; Revd Chris Russel; Mandy Ryeland; Revd Chris Smith; Clare Smith; and Danny Warnock.

Start Here

You may have asked yourself some of these questions: What is the point? Who am I? Where did I come from? Where am I heading? What happens when I die? Does this life have any ultimate meaning or purpose?

In *My Whole World Jumped*, we follow 16-year-old Dave Johnson as he grapples with the issues of everyday life: parents, girls, exams, failures, successes and the complexities of friendship. When a mysterious and anonymous CD ROM lands on his doormat, Dave is caught up in a tragic tale of family intrigue. He unexpectedly finds himself face to face with the secrets of his past and with questions about the meaning of his present and future.

My hope is that you too will be challenged by these questions as you read – and that this book might guide you to the beginnings of some answers.

I am grateful to Jonathan Brant for his work and creativity.

Nicky Gumbel, Holy Trinity Brompton

Chapter One

Tuesday 16 January, 3.15 pm

The long, blonde hair of the girl strapped into the bucket seat next to mine whipped about her beautiful face like strands of gold. I took my eyes off the road for just long enough to fire my most winning smile at her. She smiled back – adoringly.

The needle on the speedometer was dancing around the 100 mph mark as I carefully removed my hand from the small, leather-bound steering wheel of my convertible Ferrari and settled it, ever so gently, onto her bare knee. She leant across to kiss me . . .

'Fifteen minutes remain.'

The sound of the teacher's voice rudely roused me from a great daydream. Back in the real world I looked around the school hall. It was hot and stuffy as only crowded, centrally heated places can be and I slid my fingers down behind my collar trying to get some air.

The hall was set up for our mock GCSE examinations (trust my school to locate them in January, perfectly positioned to make even the Christmas holidays miserable), with row after row of neatly spaced desks each with a prisoner seated behind. With a few minutes of the exam to go only the most conscientious were still writing. The clever had finished, confident that their brilliant answers could not be improved upon, and the no-hopers had given up, unable to wring one more significant fact from their overheated brains.

'That was so unbelievably easy!'

The voice was perfectly pitched. Loud enough to be audible throughout most of the hall, quiet enough to escape the notice of the partially deaf teacher who stood with his back to us, writing instructions onto the blackboard in his swirling, old-fashioned handwriting. Due to staff shortages (and the other teacher having left to escort one of my less stable classmates on a trip to the toilet) this geriatric was the only teacher supervising our examination.

'Bring on the "A" levels, I say. They might provide at least some challenge.'

I tried to ignore Philip Squire's boasting. Perhaps I'd be lucky and he'd just shut up. I hadn't found the exam easy but that's not because I'm stupid. The sanitised version that teachers write on reports to my parents describes me as 'intelligent but under-motivated'. In class, when we've driven them to distraction, they call me 'mind-numbingly lazy'. Well, I'll scrape through, probably go on to take a couple of 'A' levels, and that should be good enough for a 16-year-old boy at Southerton Comprehensive.

I stared down at my completed paper, which was placed neatly in the centre of a desk strewn with the usual end-of-exam debris – sweet wrappers, spare pens and paper. I leant my head on my arm and stole a look to my right. Philip Squire sat next to me – unfortunately. He had stopped bragging but he still managed to look as self-satisfied and immaculate as ever. He was leaning back in his chair glancing coolly around the room at us lesser mortals. His left elbow rested on the desk and an expensive watch poked out of his sleeve. He effortlessly twirled a Mont Blanc fountain pen between his fingers – it was his most prized possession – and he looked for all the world like the successful businessman he planned to become. I leant fractionally further forward and looked down the row to where a girl with long blonde hair was sitting.

Sophie, Sophie, Sophie . . . Sophie was the object of my earlier daydream, in fact of all my dreams. Just looking at her made my insides feel warm and my hands start to sweat. I had liked Sophie, perhaps worshipped is a better word, since Year 7 and by some happy coincidence we always seemed to share a lot of classes. Not that this meant I'd ever got to know her, or even had a proper conversation with her for that matter. I'm not exactly the life and soul of a party, and while I'm not particularly shy either, the truth is that girls, especially girls I like, make me nervous. I don't think it's an uncommon problem, but it's very frustrating.

As I watched her, Sophie straightened up and placed the end of her pen in her mouth. She chewed thoughtfully for a minute and then, without warning, looked in my direction and smiled.

Instantly my insides twisted into a vicious knot, and my face contorted into what I'm sure was a hideous grimace as I tried in vain to smile back. Next to me Philip raised a hand in casual and stylish acknowledgement. I swore under my breath and sank back into my seat in anger and despair. Angry because someone as arrogant and unpleasant as Philip didn't deserve even a smile from someone as wonderful as Sophie, and despairing because I found it hard to believe that any girl, let alone a girl like Sophie, would ever waste a smile on me.

Philip Squire had been watching me.

'I don't believe it,' he whispered. 'Davey-boy Johnson's got a thing for Sophie Tanner!' I looked away, hoping that the teacher would come our way, wishing that Phil would just give it a rest. It was not to be. 'Not even in your wildest dreams, Davey,' continued Phil. 'She's way out of your league. You leave Sophie Tanner to me, Davey. I know what a girl like that wants and I think I'm just the man to give it to her. Don't you agree, Davey?'

'Time's up. Pens down,' called the teacher from the front of the hall, silencing Phil and distracting his attention so that he lost control of the precious pen he had been twirling so beautifully. The pen slipped from his hand and fell into the gangway between us. Instinctively, propelled by my anger and frustration, my foot snaked out. I'd teach Philip Squire to keep his big, ugly mouth shut. I caught the pen square on the volley just before it hit the ground. It was a strike a Brazilian centre forward would have been proud of.

Philip's mouth dropped open. The pen shot forward like a bullet. It bounced, skidded and clattered straight down the aisle. Heads bobbed up, eyes turned and the whole hall stared as the pen slid to stillness right at the teacher's feet. After the sudden noise there was silence again, every eye turned to the front.

Mr Durge rolled the offending pen over with his foot, contemplated it for a moment, then bent down and picked it up. The impact had caused the pen to leak and Mr Durge pulled a handkerchief from his pocket in an unsuccessful and irritated attempt to remove the permanent black ink from his fingers.

Mr Durge's temper is legendary. He's old almost to the point of being senile and I don't think he's ever come to terms with modern teaching practices. He still insists on calling us by our surnames, and demands that we call him sir! He comes to assemblies wearing a black cape that makes him look like Batman's decrepit grandfather and according to school rumour he can often be heard in the staff room, bemoaning the fact that caning and flogging are no longer part of a teacher's duties.

With this in our minds the entire hall froze in anticipation of the inevitable eruption. Nobody drew breath as we watched the blood drain from his face. He lifted the pen up high, held between the thumb and forefinger of a hand that trembled slightly.

'Whose pen is this?' he asked with menacing composure.

Nobody moved and the tension mounted. Philip, who I have to admit is cool under pressure, had picked up his spare pen and was looking determinedly nonchalant. My breath was short and my heart was beating madly.

Mr Durge repeated his question in a whisper of barely controlled fury. Still there was silence. In the blink of an eye Mr Durge's face turned from white to purple (and I swear there were pink and red phases in between). The quiver in his hand now ran through his entire body. He stormed up the aisle.

'Philip Squire!' He spat out the name as if it were poison. 'You stupid, arrogant little boy. Did you think I wouldn't recognise your pen? Who else would bring something like this to school?'

Philip turned to look in my direction. I started to raise my hand but was stopped by a vicious kick in the ankles from behind and simultaneously another outburst from Durge. He practically screamed at Philip.

'Look at me when I'm talking to you. What sort of infantile prank were you playing at?' Philip started to protest, but before he'd even formed the words Durge yelled, 'Shut up! You've wasted enough of our precious time. You will remain here until everyone else has left and then you and I will talk. The rest of you leave your exam papers on the desk and get out of my sight. In silence!'

I tried again. 'Please, Mr Durge, it was my . . .'

Durge turned to me. 'Silence I said. Now get out.'

'But sir . . .'

'Get out, right now – or you'll end up in detention too.'

Before I could protest further a strong hand grabbed my arm and pulled me forcefully away from my desk. As soon as we had reached the safety of the noisy and crowded hallway I turned angrily on my best friend.

'That hurt!' I bent down to massage my aching ankle.

'What?' asked Charlie, all pretend innocence.

'The kick you gave me is what. Why wouldn't you let me own up?'

'It wasn't going to make any difference.' Charlie shrugged expressively. 'Durge had his sights set on Phil. At best you'd only have ended up in detention with him and what's the point of that? I did you a favour.'

I scowled, but it was impossible to remain angry with Charlie for long; even the most foul-tempered of teachers found that.

Charlie, whose real name is long and Latin (I can't say it let alone write it), has been my best friend since we started junior school together, and his friendship makes Southerton Comprehensive bearable. 'Life and soul of the party' might not fit me, but it describes Charlie perfectly. He's invited to every party that takes place at our school. Little kids beg him in the faint hope that he might turn up and elevate their street cred for ever, and even sixth-formers know he's a good person to have on your guest list. He has more friends and would-be friends than he knows what to do with.

'Anyway, my mum keeps making me promise to look after you,' said Charlie. 'The little lost boy act you always put on when you come round really works. You've con-vinced her that you're some sweet-natured innocent who's too good for this world.'

I adore Charlie's mother, and it's true I am always on my best behaviour when I'm round at her house. It has long been my opinion that Charlie owes everything (his Mediterranean good looks, his charm and his shatterproof self-confidence) to his mother – a beautiful and stylish Italian woman. (The two of them fled from Italy to escape Charlie's father, who, according to Charlie's hints, is some kind of Mafia boss.) Apart from holding down an impressive job and cooking the most sensational pasta, she dotes on Charlie, treating him like royalty. I ask you, who wouldn't ooze self-confidence and charm with a mother like that?

Just then I caught sight of Philip Squire striding down the corridor. I called out to him but he swept past us without so much as acknowledging my existence.

'Uh-oh! Here comes trouble,' whispered Charlie as Mr Durge strode up.

'David.' The ancient teacher addressed me in too friendly a tone for the dishing out of detentions. 'I look forward to seeing you on Friday night.'

'Friday night?'

'At the chess club, of course,' said Durge. He was noticeably offended that I should have forgotten such an important event, but one term of chess club had been more than enough for me and I racked my brain for a reasonable excuse. I started to stammer something foolish before Charlie came to my rescue.

'Dave can't make it, Mr Durge.'

'What?' said Durge.

'Dave can't be there. At the chess club, that is,' Charlie added sweetly, as though someone of Durge's age might already have forgotten what they were talking about. 'You see, he's now a member of the swimming team.'

Mr Durge and I both looked at Charlie with open mouths, but while Mr Durge blustered on in that peculiarly teacherish way about correct procedure and prior commitments, I simply sat back and watched Charlie charm me out of a difficult situation, as he had done so many times in the past.

'Thanks, Charlie,' I murmured as soon as Durge was out of earshot.

'No problem,' he replied. 'Being seen around with a member of the chess club was beginning to affect even my reputation. I was serious about the swimming though.'

'Forget it. I've had it with school clubs.'

'But we need you,' said Charlie. 'The National Schools Swimming Championships take place at the end of this term.'

'Charlie, I haven't swum for years – I'd drown before I'd done a length.'

'Come on, Dave! I have just saved you from a detention and from chess club. That must count for something.'

At that moment Sophie walked down the corridor, laughing and surrounded by her usual gaggle of friends. Totally without permission, my eyes followed and lingered on her. Charlie caught the direction of my look and, knowing my feelings, took a new tack.

'Have you ever seen Sophie in a swimming costume?' asked Charlie. 'She's a member of the swimming club, you know. Great girl, but sad, lonely and unattached since she dumped that sixth-former – Rob something, wasn't it?'

'Robert Young,' I replied absent-mindedly. Sophie's social life had been a secret study area of mine for some years now.

'That's the one,' agreed Charlie. 'But now that he's out of the picture you should ask her out.'

'Charlie, I'm not interested.' Even I noticed that my voice lacked its earlier conviction and I kicked myself for it. Charlie sensed his advantage and pressed on.

'Look, no pressure. Just turn up to the first practice of term on Friday, do a few lengths, come out for a drink with a few of the guys – and girls,' he added with a very pointed look. 'Then, if you're still not interested I'll never hassle you again.'

'Well maybe,' I shrugged. 'If I'm not too busy I'll consider it, but only because I need the exercise. Not,' I tried to look meaningfully at him, 'because I'm interested in any girl.'

Charlie knew this was the best I was going to give him, so, after asking if I wanted to join him, he sprinted off to rendezvous with some other friends.

I collected my things and headed out of school. The January afternoon was cold and wet and getting darker by the minute. I was forced to dodge occasionally, trying to avoid the sheets of spray sent up by cars driving close to the kerb. It reminded me of a game Charlie and I used to play in the rain. We would gesture obscenely at lorry drivers then run full tilt, pursued by a wall of water, as they tried to drench us in spray. My friendship with Charlie never ceased to amaze me; we were so different yet understood each other so well. Perhaps it was because neither of us had any brothers or sisters around.

In previous years we would always walk home together,

but recently we had both begun to notice that our friendship was changing. Our interests were different and so, increasingly, were our friends. I'm sure neither of us wanted the friendship to fail, but I knew I had more to lose. Charlie had other friends to take my place, and his mother to confide in, but I knew that without him I would be alone.

Seeing the people I passed in the rain looking so miserable, heads bowed and their necks screwed down deep into sodden collars, amused me. I enjoyed the walk home whatever the weather. In fact, I enjoyed the walk more than I enjoyed arriving. I turned left into the small, neat close where we had lived for the past twelve years, and I looked through the gloom to our house, medium-sized and modern, almost hidden in one corner.

That night, as usual, the house stood dark. There were no lights on and no cars in the drive. My parents were out – working.

I walked through the close and glanced in at the other houses. Warm orange light escaped from living room windows, and I could see children sitting watching TV. In one house someone's mother worked in the kitchen, half-watching an Australian soap on a small portable.

I pulled a key from my pocket as I reached our drive and slipped it into the front door. The door opened into darkness and silence. 'I'm home,' I called with heavy sarcasm.

Our house always reminds me of the show home on a new housing development I once visited with my mother. Everything matched and it was equipped with every modern convenience that money can buy. Yet it was lifeless. Like a show home, you couldn't quite put your finger on it, but you knew something was missing; that it was the shell of a home and not the real thing.

I went straight to my bedroom (after a brief but vital detour through the kitchen). This was my space and even though it was a big room it was crowded with my things. My parents were fast becoming rich and a little bit of 'morning TV' psychology told me that they felt guilty about all the time they spent at work and that they tried to compensate for their guilt by giving me things. Well, I wasn't complaining! I've long been the sort of person who has crazes. For a while nothing in the world is so important as fishing, or football, or computers, and, embarrassingly, last term it was chess. Then the interest fades, usually after I've become good but not brilliant, and it's on to the next thing. My room is full of the para-phernalia of ten years of these crazes, most of it untouched for aeons but in no danger of being thrown away.

I slumped down in front of my TV, determined to waste as much time as possible before starting on revision. When I finally got up much later to get something more substantial to eat, I noticed *it*. Lying on my bed was a note and a package, obviously dropped there by my mother who reserves the right to come and go from my room as she pleases (if I am lucky, taking my dirty washing with her). The note was in her handwriting: 'Working late. Food in freezer. So sorry. Mum. PS This parcel came for you this morning.'

It was a thick brown padded envelope with a city postmark. On it, in simple handwriting, was my name and address. I didn't often get post so I was surprised and mystified. The handwritten address seemed to rule out junk mail. It took me a couple of minutes to wrestle it open: whoever had packed it had been a little over-enthusiastic with the Sellotape. There was no letter inside, in fact nothing written at all, just an unmarked CD wrapped in the kind of bubbly stuff that pops when you squeeze it.

Chapter Two

Tuesday 16 January, 8.00 pm

I turned the mysterious CD over and over in my hands and shrugged. Obviously I wasn't going to learn anything until I played it. I removed a CD from my stereo and carefully inserted the new one. The player spun to life but to my disappointment nothing appeared on the LCD display: no running time, no number of tracks, an absolute blank. I tapped the play button. Nothing happened. It was a dud. In disgust I removed the CD from my stereo and tossed it onto my bed.

After preparing and eating a microwave dinner I returned to my bedroom. As I reached out to grab the TV remote control that was lying on top of my computer another idea struck me. What if the disk wasn't an audio CD at all but a CD ROM? Excited again, I retrieved the CD from my bed and flicked the computer's power switches, tapping impatiently on my desk as it booted up. Finally the first Windows screen appeared. With the CD inserted in the disk drive I moved the mouse pointer to the correct box and double clicked. The indicator light flickered to show the drive was active and my breathing quickened. A line of flashing print appeared in the middle of the screen. What I read made my heart beat faster.

'The contents of this disk are for the eyes of David Johnson only.'

'No big deal,' I told myself. 'Any third-rate hacker can personalise the first screen of a program. It's just a clever, attention-grabbing gimmick.' I manoeuvred the mouse pointer to a small box marked 'Continue' and clicked.

I found myself looking at a little cartoon character with tousled brown hair, blue trousers and a yellow top. His lips moved and a voice spoke to me through the computer's built-in speakers. Simultaneously a line of print displaying the same words scrolled across the bottom of the screen.

'Hi, Dave. I'm going to be guiding you through this disk. Enjoy the trip! Oh, by the way, do me a favour and keep this disk a secret. Simply accept it as a gift from an unknown friend.'

I was impressed with the sound and graphics. This was pretty state-of-the-art for some freebie sent out in the post.

The guide spoke again. 'Don't just stand there! Follow me!'

I watched fascinated as the little figure turned away from me and walked into what looked like the mouth of a tunnel. Just before he disappeared into the darkness he turned and beckoned. My mouth dropped open as another cartoon figure appeared on the screen. It was me! That is, it looked like me. It had my build and colouring, my school uniform and even the battered black backpack that I always carried. The second figure also turned away and followed the guide into the tunnel.

I tore my eyes away from the screen, stood and paced with a whirling mind and a pounding heart around my bedroom. Suddenly finding yourself the subject of some unknown person's program was unsettling – like being stalked or spied on. I shuddered, but in the end curiosity got the better of me and I returned to my computer.

I punched a button to erase my screen saver and then found myself looking up the aisle from the back of a large and beautiful church, or more likely a cathedral. At first I could see little more than the bright colours and pictures of the stained-glass windows, but gradually the screen lightened, just as if my eyes were becoming accustomed to the dark, and I could see the guide sitting on a pew halfway down the church. (His cartoon body was cleverly superimposed onto the 'real life' background of the cathedral.) He was twisted around in his seat looking back at me, and just behind him sat my screen persona.

'Welcome. Beautiful place, isn't it? "Beautiful but boring," some would say and perhaps you'd agree with them? Perhaps you think places like this and even Christianity itself have nothing to offer you? Well, I hope this disk will make you think again.'

Stranger and stranger. It looked as though this CD wasn't a new game, or some clever advertising trick, but someone's way of pushing Christianity. Who would want to go to all that trouble? I didn't even know any Christians. I mean, I knew one or two people who went to church, Charlie's mum for one, but nobody serious enough to try and convert me. Religious people did sometimes come to speak at school, but as Charlie and I always spent assemblies scanning the newspaper for the previous evening's football scores I didn't listen very carefully.

What importance could religion possibly have for me? It wasn't as if I was ever going to become a vicar, and knowing all about the Bible or regularly attending church didn't seem to be of much use in other walks of life. In any case a lot of the Christian claims are too outrageous to be believed – at least that's what our RE teacher always said.

I clicked to continue.

The next level was great. Whoever the mysterious 'unknown friend' was, he or she obviously intended to entertain as well as educate me. A cartoon courtroom scene appeared, complete with packed galleries, a high imposing bench and seated behind it the ugliest and cruellest looking judge you have ever seen. The scene was animated and I watched as my character was led into the courtroom by two vicious-looking and heavily armed guards.

'The judge bears more than a passing resemblance to my boss,' said the guide as he reappeared on the screen. 'I'll be on the dole if he ever gets hold of this disk. Revenge on my boss aside, the scene does have a serious purpose. If you were dragged before a judge in a court of law, would you be willing to swear that Jesus was the Son of God and that he rose from the dead?'

I heard a car pull into the driveway and a door open then slam shut again. Seconds later I heard the distinctive clicking of my mother's high heels and the grating noise of her key in the lock. I got up and placed a towel along the bottom of my bedroom door. It was a trick I often used if I didn't want to speak to her. Thinking my light was out she'd assume I had had an early night and gone to bed. I also flicked off the speakers on the computer. From now on I would have to read what the guide had to say.

It didn't take me long to answer his question. I'm a firm believer in science (although that might surprise my teachers) and science says that death is the end. It is also clear on the fact that babies are not born to virgins (which Mary was, if you believe the script of the nativity plays). I'd done sex education, I'd watched the special videos and seen the anatomical models – I knew about that stuff! I typed my answer into the box at the bottom of the screen.

'No, I don't believe it and I certainly wouldn't swear to it.'

'OK,' said the guide. 'Now we know where we stand. However, there are millions of people who would stake their lives on Jesus and his resurrection from the dead. If you follow me I'll show you that such people have good reasons for believing as they do. Follow me, if you dare!'

With that challenge the guide disappeared. Now the screen was filled with hundreds of tiny mug shots. It made my monitor look like the 'wanted' poster outside a police station.

Using the magnifying glass from the toolbar at the top of the screen I looked more closely at the faces and I recognised some: celebrities, sportsmen and women, politicians, even some historical figures.

I clicked on the distinctive features of Freddie Mercury. His band, Queen, had been my mother's favourite and Freddie had always fascinated me, perhaps because of his early death from AIDS. When I clicked a file appeared, with a name and picture and some details about his life. I clicked again. Now there was a short quote taken from an interview shortly before his death: 'You can have everything in the world and still be the loneliest man, and that is the most bitter type of loneliness. Success has brought me world idolisation and millions of pounds, but it's prevented me from having the one thing we all need – a loving ongoing relationship.'

'So what?' I thought. 'He died a lonely and unhappy man. That's not news.' I had only to look at my parents to know that money doesn't buy happiness.

I returned to the main screen and clicked at random on an old-fashioned and fierce-looking face. 'Count Leo Tolstoy' the file told me. I'd heard of him – foreign obviously, and didn't he write a novel? Yes, according to the file he was the author of *War and Peace*, perhaps the greatest novel in world literature. I clicked for more information and read his story: 'After an incredible life where he achieved his goals in practically every area, Tolstoy was left with this one question: "Is there any meaning in my life which will not be annihilated by the inevitability of death which awaits me?"'

That was a good question, and one that hit me hard. Death was more real to me than to most people my age. It had torn my life apart once and I could never completely conquer the fear that it might happen again.

Perhaps this is as good a time as any to tell you a little about my family history. You see I wasn't always an only child. I had a sister; in fact I had a twin sister. She died in a drowning accident while we were still toddlers. Actually it's a miracle that I survived, dragged from the sea by a passing stranger.

I can still recall the tragedy clearly, if only in my recurring nightmares, but I can barely remember my sister. An aching hole and loneliness has taken her place in my life. The file informed me that in his old age Tolstoy returned to his own land with his big question still unanswered. It was there, from his own farm labourers, that he learned that only in Jesus Christ can an answer to that question be found.

Then I understood the purpose of this screen. Whoever had written it intended to convince me that non-Christians die sad and unfulfilled, while Christians find meaning and happiness. My cynicism didn't stop me thinking that I envied Tolstoy his 'answer'.

For hour after hour that night I kept reading, long after I heard my father return and go to join my mother in bed. I explored face after face, unwillingly impressed by all the different and successful people who believed in Jesus.

Finally, well after midnight, I flicked off my computer and fell into bed, too tired even to undress. In spite of my tiredness I lay awake. I was wondering if there might be a God who could make sense of this mess that people call life. In the end I rejected the idea. If God existed why had I never seen him, heard him or felt him?

Wednesday 17 January, 7.45 am

I hate my alarm clock!

In the dim morning light I leant over, trying to slap the annoying thing into silence. Eventually successful, I slid back down into my bed. Other people, particularly Charlie, complain loudly about the brutal tricks their mothers use to get them out of bed in the mornings. Mine doesn't bother: I guess she's too busy dreaming and scheming about her next big sale. Her indifference makes forgetting about school and drifting back to sleep not only attractive but possible.

I wriggled slightly, trying to get more comfortable – something was poking into my hip. What was that? As soon as I felt my belt buckle I was wide awake. Why was I still fully dressed? Memories of the previous evening, of mysterious gifts and unanswerable questions, flooded into my sleep-clouded mind. Should I skip school and continue through the disk? I decided against it: even *my* mother would be concerned if I missed school during exams. Better to play it cool and get back to it this evening.

I showered and re-dressed and arrived downstairs looking only a little more crumpled than usual.

My mother was sitting at the table in the breakfast room drinking coffee and reading the newspaper. She didn't look up as I entered the room. I had prepared myself a huge bowl of cereal and a coffee and sat down at the table before she lowered the paper and spoke to me. Not unexpectedly she began with an apology.

'Sorry I was late last night,' she said. I mumbled something around a mouthful of cereal and she changed the subject. 'How was your exam?' she asked.

'OK,' I replied. 'Not too difficult. But don't expect anything special – I hate physics.'

'It's just that you're not very good at it,' she said cheerfully. As if that was supposed to make me feel good about myself!

Now she moved onto her favourite subject – herself and her spectacular career as an estate agent. I wasn't in the mood for pretending to be interested, so the conversation had dried up and died away, and I was on my way out of the door before she remembered the package.

'Was your parcel interesting?' she asked.

Fortunately I had anticipated the question.

'It was just some freebie CD from a record company,' I lied. Adding a hasty goodbye I escaped out of the front door.

The morning passed in a blur. It was mostly boring revision periods and I should have been studying for our next exam – French – but I simply stared at my books without reading them. I was so quiet that Charlie, sitting next to me and trying to engage me in conversation, or at least to get me to listen to the account of his latest conquest (some upper-class beauty from the local private school apparently), actually thought I was ill.

At lunchtime I took my French books to the cafeteria

with me. Not because I had any intention of revising, but because it gave me an excuse to sit at a table on my own. I was finally jerked out of my reverie by the scraping sound of a chair being drawn back at my table. I looked up in annoyance. If it was one of the little kids from the lower years I was going to enjoy telling him where to go!

Sophie smiled down at me.

A hurried glance around the cafeteria revealed other empty tables. Sophie had chosen to sit with me! She had a friend with her, a popular girl called Sunita, who sat down and studied me critically. I tried to buy time and steady my shaking hands by shovelling another forkful of shepherd's pie into my mouth.

I watched Sophie carefully, while trying to appear engrossed in the important business of eating. She settled into her chair and arranged her lunch in front of her on the table, pushing her long blonde hair back behind her shoulders with one hand as she did so. Connoisseurs of the female form, Charlie for instance, do not consider Sophie beautiful. She is tall and graceful, but her figure is athletic rather than possessed of the curves that he values so highly. Even her face is a little too average to be considered beautiful. That is, until she smiles. When she smiles her whole appearance changes, her face comes alive and she's breathtaking. At least I think so.

She was smiling at me now, but in a slightly disconcerting way. A greasy, grey gob of shepherd's pie had escaped the corner of my mouth and begun a slow, leisurely descent down my chin. It left behind it a slimy trail, like a snail's.

It wasn't until Sophie kindly pointed it out that I even noticed the offending food. I felt my ears, then my forehead, then my whole face turn bright red, as still chewing I wiped my chin with the back of my hand.

After that embarrassment, 'Hi' was the best opening I could manage.

'Hi,' replied Sophie, firmly returning the ball to my court.

Even for me my next line sets records for idiocy. I don't know what I was thinking. I guess the shock of actually sitting and eating lunch with her reduced me to nursery school levels of social interaction.

'Would you like to try some shepherd's pie?' I asked Sophie, holding out a forkful.

Sunita just stared at me. I could tell she was wondering how someone so emotionally and psychologically disturbed came to be at our school. Even Sophie looked bewildered.

Fortunately she laughed as if I had made an amusing remark, and said firmly, 'No thank you!'

The conversation was going nowhere fast. Deep down I knew it was up to me to say something intelligent, but as time ticked by I just sat looking blankly over Sophie's right shoulder. Sunita looked exasperated. I think she decided that the entertainment value of this lunch period was going to be an absolute zero unless she got things moving herself.

'So you're thinking of joining the swimming club?' she said.

'Well, Charlie is trying to persuade me, but it's a long

time since I swam,' I replied. I felt ridiculously grateful to Sunita for opening up the conversation.

'Dave, you must,' said Sophie. I honestly think it was the first time I had heard her use my name, and it reduced me almost to tears because it sounded so good. 'It's so much fun,' she was continuing, 'and Charlie says you used to be very good.'

'Charlie's very kind,' I said with confidence flooding back. 'But the last time we swam together we were still wearing armbands.'

'Liar!' Sophie Tanner actually laughed at one of my feeble jokes. 'Charlie's told me all about the junior club you both swam for. He said you were really very good – much better than him.'

I was lapping this up. Charlie had obviously laid it on thick for Sophie. I loved him for it!

'He's exaggerating.' (I smiled what I hoped was a modest smile – one that implied 'It's all true, but I'm too nice a guy to admit it'.) 'What about you though? I've heard that you're the best in the club at both freestyle and backstroke.'

I was perfectly willing to turn this into a mutual admiration session if that kept Sophie at my table for one second longer. She smiled. I knew she took swimming seriously and was pleased with the compliment. For the first time ever I found myself in conversation with Sophie. We drifted from swimming to mocks and school life in general. Sunita just sat back picking at her lunch. I didn't realise it at the time, but I suppose she was waiting for someone.

The real world rushed in with a crash when another tray clattered down on our table.

Chapter Three

Wednesday 17 January, 12.55 pm

'Hi, Sophie! Hi, Nita!' said Philip Squire, ignoring me completely as he sat down. 'Thanks for saving me a place. I was delayed trying to convince Durge that only a complete and utter imbecile would be stupid enough to kick a pen at him. The old fool still won't believe it wasn't me.'

He scored a direct hit – I felt insulted and shamed at the same time. I lowered my head and played with my food. He and Sunita chattered away together. Sophie remained quiet. Whether she was absorbed in the conversation or not I wasn't sure. It didn't matter. Suddenly I had nothing more to say.

I took the coward's way out and was a full three paces away from the table before I had the confidence to turn and call out a feeble 'See you'. I was careful not to make eye contact, but it didn't stop me hearing Phil's deliberately loud voice.

'Thanks for the invitation to your party, Sophie. Of course I'll be there. You needn't have begged. You know I find you completely irresistible.'

His flirtation was received with a loud giggle, but whether it was Sunita or Sophie I couldn't tell, and didn't want to know.

The afternoon was misery. Philip and Sophie strolled into the French exam together, and Philip was smug and gloating as he took his usual place to my right. I did terribly, and made a mental note to try to be absent the day the French results were due.

At long last the afternoon was over and I was in my bedroom waiting for the computer to boot up. When the CD ROM whirred to life I clicked through to a new screen.

I was treated to another state-of-the-art animation. This time it was of a rather unusual looking chicken having a great deal of trouble attempting to cross a very busy road.

After the short cartoon a question appeared: 'Why did the chicken cross the road?'

There was a box for me to type my answer. I put in my favourite: 'To show his friends he had guts!'

'Very funny!' said the guide as he reappeared on my screen.

'Do you know that the correct, or perhaps I should say original, answer is: to get to the other side? It's not a great joke – I know diseases that are funnier. However, "Why?" is always a good question and it's one that you should be asking. During the last level you read about people who call themselves Christians. The question now is "WHY?" Why do they believe what they do? (You have my full permission to take this disk outside and shoot it, just to put it out of its misery, if the answer it gives isn't better than the answer to the joke.)'

As the guide spoke, a succession of images began to flash up on the blue background behind him. They were all pictures of one man.

'Above all else,' said the guide, 'Christians believe what they do because of the life, death and resurrection of Jesus of Nazareth.'

The guide disappeared and was replaced by another cartoon character. This one was obviously supposed to be Russian, with fur hat, Slavic features, military uniform. He was reading from a big red book. I could see the title on the front cover: *Communist Dictionary.*

In a Russian accent he solemnly read an entry: 'Jesus Christ – a mythical figure who never existed.'

Another character, an academic or professor of some type, strode onto the screen and rudely shoved the Russian to one side. 'Fool,' he said, turning towards me and removing his little half-moon glasses. 'No serious historian, such as my learned self, would ever doubt the genuine, factual existence of Jesus of Nazareth. His life is attested to not only by the New Testament of the Christian Bible, which is itself an immensely reliable document, but also by historians of the time, both Roman and Jewish. So my boy,' he looked sternly at me, 'never doubt that Jesus really did live.'

The guide returned immediately after this little lecture.

'You see, Dave, Christians are Christians not because they believe that Jesus existed, but because they believe he was more than just a man – that he was and is God.'

Pangs of hunger reminded me that it was time to eat, and, surprise, surprise, I hadn't heard either of my parents come in. I decided that it was time to visit the kitchen. As I made my way downstairs I wondered why Christians had to rock the boat, and make themselves look so stupid, by buying into all that 'Son of God' stuff.

I pushed open the kitchen door and was surprised to find my mother standing at the stove stirring something in a saucepan.

'Hi, Mum. I didn't hear you come in.'

'I got in about half an hour ago. A possible buyer cancelled a viewing. How was school?'

'Dire. The French exam was awful.' After a moment's silence my churning thoughts spilled out into a question. 'Mum, who do you think Jesus was?'

She was startled enough to stop her stirring and turn around to look at me.

'Why do you ask?'

'I'm not really sure; it's just something I've been thinking about. I'd like to know what you think,' I coaxed her.

'Well,' she began slowly, 'it's not something I give a lot of thought to these days. When you were little we all went to church. I'm afraid, though, that after what happened to our family,' (that was the closest she ever came to referring to my twin's death), 'I can no longer believe in a loving God. So . . . maybe Jesus was just a good man . . . I don't know.'

'I see.'

To my surprise I found myself enjoying this rare moment of intimacy. Your relationship with your parents is a strange thing. My mum might think that I was an under-achiever, as she put it; she might ignore me most of the time; she might even let it slip on occasions that she wished my sister had lived instead of me – but I still loved her. And there was still something deep within me that longed for us to be close. I even considered telling her more about the disk and its contents, but just at that moment the phone rang and she ran off to answer it, leaving me with a saucepan to stir.

When she returned, her mind was full of her phone call, and she didn't talk to me. The moment had passed, and it wasn't long before I was back in my bedroom with a tray of food for my dinner.

'Imagine a new teacher arriving at a school,' said the guide. 'The school is failing – an educational disaster area. Unlike the rest of the zombies and wannabe dictators the school employs, this new man is dynamic. He's interesting, he's brilliant and he cares about students, not just about results. The girls fancy him and in time the boys start talking and dressing like him. In short, he's the best thing that's happened to the school since they started serving chips in the cafeteria.

'Then it happens. In the middle of Wednesday morning assembly he stands to his feet and announces: "I am the bread of life. Whoever comes to me will never go hungry." There's a stunned silence. Ms Frittle, the tone-deaf music mistress who has a bit of a thing for the new teacher, is so shocked that her mouth drops open and her false teeth fall out.

'The new teacher hasn't finished though. Turning to Form 10C, the biggest bunch of delinquents in the school, he declares: "I am the light of the world. Whoever follows me will never walk in darkness." The headmaster's notes drop to the floor with a crash and the first of many giggles ripples around the room.

'Still the new teacher is not finished. "I am the resurrection and the life. He who believes in me will live even though he dies; and he who lives and believes in me will never die." By now the school secretary is on the phone to the nearest mental hospital and the head of Year 7 is quietly ushering the petrified eleven- and twelve-year-olds out of the fire exit. Unconcerned, the new teacher turns to where the PE teachers are seated. "Your sins are forgiven," he says.

'That is actually not too different from what happened to Jesus' followers 2,000 years ago,' continued the guide. 'They thought they had found this wonderful, wise teacher and suddenly he started making the most outrageous claims. Many people like to think of Jesus as a "good and wise man" but he claimed to be much, much more than that.

'No normal person would say the things Jesus did, and so we are left with three options. He could have been a madman – spouting nonsense like the psychiatric patient who thinks he's Napoleon. He could have been a bad man or a con man making outrageous claims to impress people and part them from their money. If he was neither of those things then what he said must have been true and he must have been the God-man. God come to us as a man.

'Here's why Christians believe that is the correct answer . . .'

Once again the screen flickered, throwing up image

after image of Jesus. Soon they were changing so fast that it was like looking down a kaleidoscope. From the terribly tacky to the intensely beautiful, some centuries old and priceless, some new and mass-produced, each picture was in some way haunting. I began to think how remarkable it was that this poor, uneducated man from a tiny Middle Eastern country had had such a profound effect on the history of our world. While I was thinking, the kaleidoscope slowed, then stopped, and I found myself looking at a new screen.

There was a central box still flashing up image after image of Jesus. Below it was written the question: 'Jesus of Nazareth – mad, bad or God?' From the middle ran three lines, each leading to another box. These were labelled 'His Teachings', 'His Deeds', 'His Character'.

It was obviously up to me to do some exploring.

Each box asked a question, a variation of 'Are these the teachings/deeds/characteristics of a mad man or a bad man?' The guide used video clips, still pictures, quotes and other multimedia effects to make his points, then finished with some summaries.

'*Teachings*. If Jesus is a mad man or a bad man then the world has really been taken for a ride – much of our civilization and many of our laws are based upon what he taught.

'*Deeds*. Con men flourish where there is wealth. What mad man or bad man would spend his time with the poor and the neglected, offering love and hope to people who were alone and in pain and had nothing to give him?

'*Character*. Jesus' life was so perfect that even his

mother and brothers came to worship him, and his past was so clean that even his worst enemies, desperate to destroy him, couldn't find any skeletons hidden in his closet.'

I cringed at the thought of some of the stories my mother could wheel out to prove that I was far from perfect. At the merely embarrassing end of the scale was the time Charlie and I were almost expelled from primary school because we decided it would be fun to swap clothes. Unfortunately we proceeded to make the exchange, stripping all the way down to our red and blue 'Superman' Y-fronts, right in the middle of a maths class. More seriously, I had once been caught shoplifting and driven home by the local police. That didn't please my parents at all.

Jesus must have been quite a man if even his family could believe that he was God.

Thursday 18 January, 8.00 pm

Charlie appeared on my doorstep the following evening. He claimed that he wanted to revise for our final two exams. I didn't believe a word of it.

'So?' I asked, as he threw himself down on my bed.

'So what?'

He poked his foot at the tray that sat on the floor near the bottom of my bed. On it were the remains of last night's meal. Charlie eyed it with suspicion. He looked as if he were afraid that the brown sludge might suddenly jump up off the plate and attack him. 'What was that?'

'Not all of our mothers have cordon bleu qualifications. Anyway, don't change the subject. Tell me why you're here,' I said, exasperated. 'And you can save that revision excuse for my parents. You haven't even bothered to bring any books with you.'

'All right,' said Charlie. 'Calm down. Anybody would think I was distracting you from something important.'

'Perhaps you are,' I replied loftily. 'I have my own life you know.'

'Since when?' enquired Charlie. Then he had to duck to avoid the fistful of dirty underwear I flung across the room at him. 'Actually, you're right. I didn't come to revise. I came to bring you this.' He pulled a grubby square of paper out of the back pocket of his jeans and began to unfold it, finally smoothing it out on top of the bed. 'It's a "Parents' Agreement Form",' he explained. 'You have to get your mum or dad to sign it tonight, then you can hand it in to the coach at school tomorrow and then you can go to the swimming practice in the evening.'

'You really enjoy running my life, don't you?' I said.

But I took the form and Charlie refused to leave until my mother had signed it.

We settled down to spend the rest of the evening listening to music and talking about girls. Well, Charlie talked; I just listened.

Around 9.30 we were interrupted by the cheerful tune of his mobile phone. A text message awaited him.

'R U cming or wot? B here n 5 or im gon . . . 4ever! :-('

'Oops,' said Charlie. 'I'd forgotten about her. Still, she's too posh for me. I'm better off without her.'

'You can't just leave her waiting wherever it is you're sup-posed to have met her,' I protested. I knew Charlie well enough to get the picture without needing an explanation.

'No time,' shrugged Charlie. 'She said she'd be gone in five minutes. It'd take me at least three times that to get there.'

'You have a phone, Charlie!'

'But no credit. In fact if I don't find some money soon the company is going to cut me off altogether.'

That was typical of Charlie. He loved his phone for the way it looked but had no idea how to use it properly. He would waste an entire £20 call voucher on one long con-versation with the girl of the moment and then have to go for weeks without the credit to make calls. I didn't even have a mobile phone. I used to have one, but after receiv-ing a particularly horrendous bill my mother threw a fit and cancelled the contract.

In the end, Charlie made the call from the phone in my room. The conversation wasn't pretty to witness.

'Ouch,' said Charlie with a grimace, when he put the phone down. 'I think I'd better stay clear of the grammar school for a while.'

Friday 19 January, 4.00 pm

'Was Jesus just a wise teacher? No way! Was he a bad man or a mad man? Of course not! So, what was he? Who is he? For the clues and the evidence to answer those ques-tions we must turn to the key event upon which all of Christianity is founded.'

After two torturous exams I had walked home as quickly as I could. I wasn't sure whether the guide was a good teacher or I was being an unusually good student, but either way I was desperate to finish the disk before I had to leave for the swimming practice.

'This final section contains no clever graphics or multi-media effects. Let's just talk about Jesus' physical resurrection from the dead.

'Did you know that everyone agrees that Jesus' tomb was empty three days after he was executed by the authorities? That's a generally acknowledged fact. The question is: Where did the body go?

'Perhaps Jesus didn't die? As if! It was rough, tough Roman soldiers in charge of the execution – not the local Girl Guide troop. If they performed an execution and said someone was dead, then that someone stayed dead!

'Maybe Jesus' friends stole the body? Not likely! Matching Jesus' disciples against the soldiers guarding the tomb would have been like sending Mr Bean into the ring against Mike Tyson. In any case, almost all of Jesus' disciples were later killed for their belief in him and his resurrection. Even if they had managed to out-think or out-fight the guards, only very strange people indeed would die for a hoax they themselves had set up.

'What if the authorities hid the body? Impossible! The authorities hated the stories that suggested Jesus had risen from the dead. If they had had the body they would have thrown the smelly, decomposing mess down on the floor right in front of Jesus' friends. A corpse would certainly have shut them up – no more resurrection stories after that!

'As if the empty tomb isn't enough of a headache for those who want to disprove the resurrection, they also have to try to explain away the appearances of Jesus – alive and well – to his friends. We're not talking about one or two fleeting, night-time sightings reported by neurotic old women or drunk young men. Jesus appeared to over 550 different people over a six-week period. During this time he held long conversations with his friends, allowed people to touch him and even ate – not normal behaviour for ghosts or hallucinations!

'After the tomb was found empty and Jesus had made his appearances, the belief that he had been raised from the dead spread through the world faster than fire through a fireworks factory. Wherever the story of his resurrection was told, people became Christians and new churches were started.

'There is more evidence for Jesus' resurrection,' said the guide. 'Not only did the first disciples meet him and know him after he had been crucified, but also countless millions of people from every country of the world have known him in the centuries since then.

'I would like to tell you something about myself, though probably not as much as you would like to know. Although I can only allow you to see my cartoon image, I am a real person. A few years ago my life was a mess. Then somebody told me much of what I have shown you on this disk. I had nothing to lose and so I decided to see if becoming a Christian would make any difference to my life. It did, but not in the way I expected. I expected to try to live by the rules Jesus taught. Instead I actually met

Jesus. I know he was raised from the dead because, although I've never physically seen or touched him, I know him.

'I hope that what you have seen on this disk makes you wonder if Jesus might be more than just a good man. I hope you now think it possible that he was not a bad man or a mad man, but actually God living on earth as a man. I am praying right now to the Jesus I know is alive, and asking that one day you might actually meet him.'

'THE END.' The two words appeared in big, black, block capitals at the bottom of the screen.

I leant back into my chair. I had been so intrigued by the contents of the disk that for some time the 'Who?' question had slipped my mind. Now it was back. That last section had been such a personal appeal, so passionate, that I felt sure it had to be from someone who knew me. Who on earth could it be?

On the computer screen the guide remained frozen. There was something odd, incomplete, about the guide's stance. It seemed a strange pose to end on. I looked more closely. What was it about the pose that seemed wrong? Then I saw it. The guide's mouth was still open, as if he was still talking when the program ended. I moved the mouse pointer to the guide's face, positioned it over his mouth and clicked. The guide spoke again.

'Sharp eyes, Dave. I wasn't sure if you'd catch my little clue. Well, here we are. I have a feeling I am going to end up kicking myself for this little bit of honesty, but here goes anyway . . .

'Although you don't know me, I know you. I created

this disk because I could think of nothing in the world that I could give to you that is as valuable as this information. If you have any questions concerning the contents of this disk (please not about me) then you may leave a message at this email address – cat@net-csd.com – and I will get some more information to you. Goodbye, Dave.'

Now the screen was blank and the disk really was finished. Numbed by what I had just read, I flicked off the computer and looked at my watch.

It was time to go swimming.

Chapter Four

Friday 19 January, 6.30 pm

The ancient building was grey and grim, just as I remembered it. Cold and ugly, it couldn't compete with pleasure lagoons and wave machines, and now it was used only by clubs. I pushed through the heavy swing doors and was struck by the smell of chlorine and the echoes of children shouting. A whistle blew.

'Southerton Comprehensive,' I told the woman behind the window before she had a chance to demand money.

'You're early,' she said. 'But go right in.'

I pushed through the stiff and creaking turnstile. Through the windows straight ahead I could see young children splashing towards the edge of the pool. The whistle blew again and they hurried faster, scared of angering the lifeguard. I turned right and entered the men's changing rooms. It was strange to be back. The room was empty, the children were changing elsewhere, and nothing had altered: cold, wet floor; benches and hooks against the walls; a few lockers, but never enough, clustered in the centre of the room. I stripped off my school uniform, balling it up and stuffing it into a locker.

I walked through the freezing and disgusting footbath to the poolside. The guards were unravelling the long lane markers, reeling them off drums and leaving them to float in the water.

'Mind if I get in?' I called to the nearest.

'That's the general idea,' he called back. I ignored his sarcasm.

After what had happened to my twin, and nearly to me, you probably think I should have a phobia about water. Well, I don't. Perversely I've always loved it and found it comforting and relaxing. It's too long ago for me to remember if my parents made me join the swimming club that Charlie and I used to be part of, or if it was just something I wanted to do. Either way, ever since then I have loved swimming and the water. I tried to remember the short-lived craze that had meant my leaving the swimming club all those years ago. I couldn't even remember what it was.

It had been a long time, but as soon as I sliced through the surface and found myself in the familiar blue and weightless world I mentally thanked Charlie for persuading me to come.

I lost track of time as I swam, enjoying the solitude and freedom of being underwater. Only coming up when I needed to breathe, I dived and twisted and somersaulted, or floated on my back looking up at the sparkling line where water met air. After one particularly graceful manoeuvre, I broke the surface to the sound of raucous laughter. I blinked the water out of my eyes, realising that the poolside was now crowded with people. Closest to the water was Philip Squire, surrounded by his friends.

'Well, Davey boy, I never knew you were such a water

baby!' I continued to float, helpless, too breathless even to speak. 'Trouble is, Davey, you're in the wrong place. Synchronised swimming is somewhere else. Mind you, a nose-clip and some make-up would certainly improve your face.'

I floated, bobbing up and down, helpless as a rubber duck in a bath. I was embarrassed and angry but there was nothing I could do. The audience was loving the show, whooping and laughing in support of Phil's witticisms. Now that he had me at his mercy he obviously intended to exact revenge.

Fortunately for me, Charlie arrived on the scene with his usual explosion of energy. Leaping out of the changing room door, an old habit of his to avoid touching the footbath, he caught sight of me in the water. Shoving his way through the crowd, he jumped in to join me.

Charlie's arrival turned the tide for me. Philip has his friends and his admirers, but everyone loves Charlie, and his endorsement was all I needed to be welcomed as a valuable member of the swimming club. From that moment on there were no more jokes at my expense. Even the fact that I was wearing a rather tasteless pair of Bermuda shorts in place of competitive swimwear (at least they covered my private parts better than what the other boys were wearing), and that as a newcomer I was relegated to the slow lanes with the coughing, choking, splashing eleven-year-olds, escaped comment.

The practice passed quickly, and I rather enjoyed the drudgery of slogging up and down, stroke after stroke, length after length. I didn't even mind being screamed at by coaches, or constantly bumped by little kids coming the other way with their eyes tight shut and mouths wide open. As I gained confidence, I overhauled other swimmers with greater and greater regularity. The coaches' yells became less critical and more encouraging and I realised that I was doing well.

Charlie and I changed quickly and rushed off after practice. He was in high spirits, loudly congratulating himself on having unearthed a prodigy. 'I can't believe you haven't swum in six years,' he kept saying to me. 'Tell you what, I'll buy you a coke – to celebrate your return.'

On any given Friday evening, probably half the students of Southerton Comprehensive darken the doors of McDonald's, either as paid staff, paying customers or penniless hangers-on. In the past this had meant that for Charlie and other 'A-list' personalities the order was often supplemented by free fries or sundaes, but new management had taken over and such perks were history.

We secured the best booth on offer – not much graffiti, few cigarette burns and well out of sight of the senior staff – and were sitting and eating by the time the other swimmers arrived. I took the opportunity to ask Charlie a question that had been on my mind throughout the evening.

'Is it possible to trace an email address back to a real person?'

'Have you ever seen me in an anorak?' Charlie demanded in a deeply grieved voice. 'Do I look like a computer geek? I wouldn't even know how to turn a computer on if "computer lab" hadn't been made compulsory last year. You should be asking Natasha, not me,' he added, pointing to the queue.

If Charlie and I were intelligent but under-motivated, and Phil and Sophie definitely qualified as brains, then Natasha was the year's genius. She stood in line now, alone, reading a technical magazine and wearing her usual outfit of baggy army surplus clothing.

'Try Natasha,' repeated Charlie. 'She could probably teach Bill Gates a thing or two about computers. Anyway, who are you trying to track down? Don't tell me you're two-timing Sophie with some "virtual babe" you met surfing the Net!'

I didn't bother to explain to Charlie the logical impossibility of two-timing someone you had no earthly chance of one-timing in the first place, especially as Sophie herself was fast approaching our table.

'Mind if I sit down?' she asked.

'Not at all,' replied Charlie, quickly sliding around so that the only available arc of moulded plastic seating was next to me. 'But before you do, you wouldn't go and ask Natasha to join us, would you?' Sophie disappeared again and Charlie winked at me. 'Not only will uncle Charlie get your question answered for you, but an extra body will make it much more cosy on the seat!'

Sophie and Natasha returned and sat down in completely the wrong order as far as Charlie was concerned. Before he could come up with some hair-brained excuse for shuffling the seating arrangements, I turned to Natasha. She had purchased a Happy Meal solely to acquire the cheap little plastic toy – apparently they were considered something of a prize by her intelligentsia friends. Charlie and I greedily divided the tiny burger and fries while she drank the coke.

'How much do you know about email and the Internet?' I asked her.

'Enough,' she replied with total self-confidence.

Charlie cut in. 'Could you do some detective work and find someone for Dave – just from their email address?'

'That should be possible,' said Natasha. 'At a price.'

'I'll buy you a Happy Meal,' I suggested hopefully. 'Just tell me which toys you're still missing.'

'That should cover it,' she said, fishing a notebook and pen from deep inside her Norwegian army issue jacket. 'Give me the mysterious address then.' I wrote it down immediately, surprising myself with my feat of memory. 'All right. I'll give it a go. See you Monday.'

'I think she likes you, Dave,' said Sophie once Natasha was out of earshot.

'Too right,' added Charlie. 'It cost me a tenner just to get a couple of homework answers out of her. She wouldn't save her gran from a fire for a Happy Meal. It must be love. Three-timer,' he added under his breath.

Sophie overheard and looked enquiringly at him, but to my relief didn't ask the obvious question. Instead she left to join Sunita and Philip at another table.

'What's going on between her and Phil?' I managed to ask Charlie without too much of a tremor in my voice.

'Absolutely nothing for you to worry about,' he assured me.

I tried hard to believe him, but in the end couldn't. It

would be just my luck to have to watch the woman I loved going around with my worst enemy.

Monday 22 January, 6.20 am

I had passed most of the weekend locked in my room, brooding. I worked my way through the CD ROM again and found it even more fascinating the second time around. I couldn't decide what question I should email to my mysterious correspondent. I was certain I wanted to contact them again, and determined to find out who had gone to all the effort of creating the disk just for me. What I needed was a really good, really intelligent question to email them – something that they would definitely want to reply to.

On the Sunday night I had my nightmare again. As usual it was a terrifying and sweaty experience. I had been only two years old at the time of the tragedy, but the event was so traumatic that, while I can remember nothing else from that early period of my life, I have very real memories of the minutes that preceded my sister's drowning. In my dreams these memories were distorted, slightly differently each time, by the addition of certain nightmare elements – waves as big as houses, or total blackness even though the drowning had occurred during the day. I had suffered with these nightmares at least a couple of times a month for as long as I could remember. They always left me exhausted, with the sheets tangled around me and my head bursting with a splitting headache. They also left me depressed, freshly and painfully reminded of the tragic and unnecessary accident that had claimed my sister's life and left me all but alone.

While I lay in bed, still in a black and brooding mood and waiting for my alarm to go off, I thought about death. Not the ideal subject matter for a teenager's thoughts on a cold, dark, winter Monday morning. Much later, as the first grey daylight filtered into my room through the curtains, I remembered that the CD had claimed that Jesus was the answer to questions about death. But that didn't make any sense to me now. I mean, he died too, didn't he?

Feeling rather proud of myself for thinking it up, I sent my question to the email address before I left for school.

'I hate death,' I typed. 'I hate it because it gets us all in the end – and because it gets some so much sooner than others. If Jesus really was God, then why did he have to die just like the rest of us?'

In the term of the National Schools Gala, swimming practices were held an unprecedented three times a week: Mondays, Wednesdays and Fridays from 7.00 to 8.30 pm. On Monday evening I was back inside the cold, echoing swimming pool and I could tell that things were different. People were treating me with new respect, not just because Charlie and I had arrived together this time, but because of my performance at the last practice. As soon as he saw us, the senior coach, Mr Bishop, came over and told me that I'd been promoted to the intermediate lanes, and that if things continued to go well he would consider moving me up to be with the senior competition swimmers like Charlie.

I was pleased and set out swimming as strongly as I could, glad at the very least to be free of the floundering eleven-year-olds who had hampered my progress last time. The practice went well and just before the end the coach beckoned me out of the water.

'You swim really well, Dave. I'm impressed, and I think it's time for you to move up.' I could sense other eyes watching us and Charlie had sidled up alongside me, so I tried to look cool and not too eager to please. 'Am I right in thinking that breaststroke would be your number one stroke?' continued Mr Bishop. Charlie's eyes lit up but I glared at him, willing him to keep silent. This was not the time for one of his favourite sexual innuendoes. I nodded at the coach. 'Then I'm going to put you in with Philip Squire, who is our best swimmer in that stroke. I'm sure he'll take you under his wing.'

Under his wing! Philip's face made it perfectly clear, when the coach took me over to him a moment later, that he'd like to take me under all right – and keep me there until I stopped breathing. He managed a smile though (for Mr Bishop's benefit) and promised to do his best.

Time trials marked the end of every practice. They started at the coach's command and you simply swam as far and as fast as you could before the whistle sounded again. As everyone took their places in the water (there could be no diving in a pool that crowded) Phil made sure that he was right next to me and took pains to explain what was about to happen. He seemed to be taking his job seriously.

As the coach shouted for quiet and asked everyone to 'take their marks' Phil started gently edging forward in the water. The whistle blew, Phil lunged forward and thrust back his legs in a driving, frog-like, breaststroke leg kick. His right foot caught me square in the stomach (although I suspect he was aiming a little lower), winded me and forced me back against the wall. By the time I recovered the coach was screaming at me, 'Get a move on, Dave!'

I forced my lungs to work and pushed violently off from the wall, swimming like a man possessed, anger driving me to work my still-winded body harder than it could stand. It was no use. After three lengths I was exhausted. While I'd overtaken some people, Phil and the faster swimmers were still far ahead. Defeated, I relaxed and swam on as smoothly as I could until the whistle stopped us. Once I had clambered out Phil and the coach walked towards me.

'Good swim, Dave,' said Phil, smiling like an angel just as the coach arrived.

'Yes, well done, David,' echoed Mr Bishop. 'It will be a while though before Phil's worrying about his place on the team.' He clapped Phil on the back and they walked off together, leaving me dreaming of Philip Squire's humiliation.

Thursday 25 January, 8.40 pm

Three days passed without my receiving any communication from either Natasha, who seemed to be avoiding me, or the mystery person. Then on Thursday evening, as I half-heartedly went through my routine of checking for emails, the little box popped up to tell me, 'You have new messages.'

'Hi, Dave. It was great to get your email, and I'll try to answer your question.

'At first glance Jesus' death looks like the one blot on his record. So why is it so important?'

'So much for small talk,' I thought. It seemed that my mysterious correspondent was determined to keep our communications focused on business. I continued reading.

'Imagine bringing a girlfriend home to meet your parents. At first they're relieved – a decent proportion of her body is covered by her clothes, there are no metal rings poking out of her lip or nose, no studs stapled to her tongue, and, if they're not very much mistaken, she just managed to string a sentence together. "She's a real catch!" they think. But then they see it. Hanging from a chain around her neck is a tiny silver model of an electric chair, complete with ready-fried prisoner sitting in it! "Psycho alert!" they panic. What kind of girl hangs an instrument of execution around her neck?

'Crucifixion was one of the cruellest methods of execution ever devised. Why do normal people wear crosses around their necks? Why is the cross the symbol of the Christian faith? Because the cross is the greatest ever demonstration of God's love for us, and because it is the answer to the most terrible problem that has ever faced humankind.

'What problem? I hear you ask . . . The problem is sin.'

'Here we go,' I thought. This was much more what I would have expected from a religious type. I read on.

'Sin might seem like a strange idea to you, but it's simply the word the Bible uses to describe all of the wrong things we do. If you tell a secret you had promised to keep – that's sin. If you let down a friend you had sworn to stand by – that's sin. If you gossip about a classmate, and perhaps exaggerate the truth to better the story – that's sin. Now I imagine you might be saying, "Those are hardly major crimes – I'm a lot better than some people and no worse than most!" You're right. If you were to walk downstairs and pick up your mother's paper from beside the toaster . . .'

Hey, wait a minute! How did this person, quite likely a religious nut, know that every morning my mum read the newspaper over breakfast and then left it lying beside the toaster for the rest of the day? Was that such a common practice that it was just a lucky guess? Or were they, intentionally or otherwise, letting slip just how well they knew me and my family?

'. . . you would find it filled with stories of people who have committed horrible crimes. There is no doubt that if you were to compare yourself only with mass murderers and child abusers you would look good. However, sin has consequences for all of us. Sin makes us unclean. It clutters up our lives with junk, leaving us feeling guilty and dead on the inside.

'Sin also separates us from God. The rubbish and the clutter form a barrier between us and God. There is nothing that we can do to climb over or burrow under this barrier.'

I thought back to the first night after I had received the CD ROM. I remembered lying in bed wishing for a God who could make sense of my life and of the world. It had seemed like an exciting idea at the time but I had dismissed it because I simply couldn't believe it. I couldn't make myself feel God. I was now being told that there was a reason for that. It was my sin, the wrong things I had done through my life, that separated me from God.

'Now let me try to explain what Jesus' death on the cross has to do with your sin. I once heard a true story about the Auschwitz concentration camp during World War Two. In response to an escape from the camp, it was decided by the commandant that ten prisoners should be buried alive in a special concrete bunker and left until they died of starvation. The prisoners stood in line all day, waiting in terror as the German commandant and his assistant chose those who would die. When the commandant pointed at him, one man cried out in despair, "My poor wife and children!"

'At that moment a small man with round wire glasses stepped forward. "What do you want?" shouted the commandant. "I am a Catholic priest; I want to die for that man. I am old, he has a wife and children . . . I have no one," said the short man, Father Maximilian Kolbe. "Accepted," said the commandant and moved on.

'After two weeks in the starvation bunker, the priest was still alive and conscious. Normally the men starving in the bunker would tear each other apart in their fear and hunger, but under Father Maximilian's influence they sang and prayed instead. In the end Father Maximilian was taken out and killed by a lethal injection.

'Forty years later, 150,000 people gathered in St Peter's Square, Rome. Among the crowd was the man who'd been saved by Father Maximilian's death. His wife, his children and his children's children were also there. When the Pope addressed the crowd and spoke of Father Maximilian's death, he said, "This was a victory won over all the systems of contempt and hate in human beings – a victory like that won by our Lord Jesus Christ."

'In the same way that Father Maximilian stepped forward to save another man, Jesus stepped forward and gave himself up to die on the cross as our substitute. You see, in the Old Testament of the Bible the Jewish people had a way to deal with their sins. The sinner would buy, or select from his flocks, the most perfect sheep or goat he could find, then he would place his hands on the animal and confess his sins. Believing that his sins were then transferred to the animal, the animal would be killed, taking away the sin. The writers of the New Testament recognised that these animals were only a picture of the one perfect sacrifice that would take away people's sins once and for always. Jesus, the only person ever to have lived a perfect life, died as a substitute for us. He took on himself all of the wrong we have done. His blood can remove the rubbish and clutter of our sin and make our lives clean again.

'The truth is that the cross, and particularly the exact way it works, is a mystery. We will never understand precisely what happened when Jesus died in our place, but what is important is the result. Fortunately you don't have to understand how the internal combustion engine works in order to drive a car, and we don't have to understand perfectly how the cross works to benefit from it.

'There is one story that Jesus told that I love more than any other. It is normally called the Parable of the Prodigal Son. It is a good illustration of the result of what happened on the cross. In this story a young man demands that his father give him his inheritance. He then runs away from home, wasting his money on all that is worthless. Eventually he finds himself broke, hungry and unhappy. He dreams of his life at home and thinks that perhaps, in spite of everything, his father might just take him back as a servant. With this slight hope in his heart he sets off for home. When he finally arrives, he sees his father at the door of the house. To his shock his father starts towards him, then breaks into a run, then throws himself on his son, hugging and kissing him and welcoming him home.

'What happened to the Prodigal Son can happen to us. Jesus' death on the cross destroyed the barrier that separates us from our Father God. If we acknowledge the wrong we have done, and recognise that Jesus' death on the cross can cleanse us from it, then we can come back to the Father and experience his love.

'The problem was sin. The answer that God came up with was Jesus' death on the cross. That's why Jesus had to die!'

A prayer was printed on the email but I skimmed over it and looked down to the final couple of lines.

'Dave, you live with your father, but I don't and can't. Maybe that is why the story of the Prodigal Son means so much to me. Knowing that I have a Father in heaven who loves me has changed my life. Look, let me come clean. I know why you hate death so much. I know who you lost and I know how you lost her. But don't let that stop you. Go for it, Dave – try this out. You've got nothing to lose.'

That was the end of the email.

I pushed myself away from my desk so hard that I slid three-quarters of the way across the room on my wheeled desk chair. I was almost tearing my hair out with the frustration of not knowing who was sending me these things. Nobody but nobody outside of the closest family and friends knew about my twin and what had happened to her.

At that moment my phone rang. I picked it up.

'Yeah?' I grunted.

'I hope you have the money for a Happy Meal, Dave.'

I was silent, totally confused.

'Dave,' the voice tried again, 'it's Natasha, and I think I've found your mystery person.'

Chapter Five

Monday 29 January, 4.15 pm

Charlie and I closeted ourselves in my bedroom, armed with a phone number. When Natasha had claimed she had found my man, she had been exaggerating. It still cost me a Happy Meal though, and what's worse, she insisted that I waste a Saturday morning and accompany her to McDonald's to eat it. Charlie was still convinced that she fancied me.

For Natasha, the investigation had been easy; the only difficulty had been tearing herself away from her books for long enough to do the research. In the email address was all the information she needed. Now to me that list of letters and dots meant absolutely nothing, but then I'm no genius. That is why I 'employed' Natasha. She recognised that the address belonged to a commercial company and she knew that csd.com would be its address on the Internet. She simply logged on and there was all the information she needed. That was when she called me.

'Now that we know the company, its address and its phone number,' she said, 'it should be simple to find the employee who logs on under the name "CAT".'

Unfortunately she was wrong. It was far from simple.

Desperate for a bit of moral support I had let Charlie in on a little of what was going on. He was thrilled with the situation, excited to find something that could distract him from the tedium of schoolwork.

With Charlie's encouragement I took a deep breath and dialled.

'Good afternoon, Creative Software Designs,' said the lady on the switchboard.

'Um . . . hello,' I faltered. Charlie dug me in the ribs and gave me a 'get on with it' look. 'I was just wondering,' I tried again, 'if you could tell me the real name, or put me through to the employee who calls himself "CAT".' There was silence on the other end of the line.

'I'm sorry,' she said after a moment. 'I'm not allowed to give out any personal information about our employees. Goodbye.'

The line went dead. Charlie was undeterred. He persuaded me that we should take turns ringing up, putting on a different voice and accent each time. First he asked to speak to 'CAT'. Then when that didn't work I asked for Charles, then he asked for Craig, then Carl. We would have kept on for as long as we could think of names beginning with 'C' if the receptionist hadn't quickly caught on and threatened to call the police.

Finally, we decided that the only possible solution was to visit the company's offices and make some face-to-face enquiries. A little map work uncovered their location, fortunately only about a 40-minute train ride away.

Tuesday 30 January, 3.45 pm

The weather was on our side. An exceptionally hard frost meant that our games periods were cancelled. The ground was too hard even for the torture of cross-country running. We responsible GCSE students were sent home to get on with some coursework or revision. Charlie and I jumped on the first train for the city.

When we arrived, we found an old office block, half-falling down and looking distinctly non-high-tech. However, there was a bright and shiny sign with the name 'Creative Software Designs' emblazoned on it. It was our bad luck that there was also a security guard who refused to let us into the building. We retreated to the bus stop across the road and settled down to wait. I hoped to see someone I recognised.

We discovered that the only thing more boring than sitting at a bus stop waiting for a bus is sitting at a bus stop not waiting for a bus. It was a very unpleasant location for a spying operation. The freezing January wind cut through every stitch of clothing we were wearing, and on the frequent occasions that buses pulled into the stop we were all but choked by the disgusting fumes they pumped out.

The afternoon dragged by but by seven in the evening, having sat around for nearly three hours, we had not seen anything unusual or anyone we recognised. We doubted that there was anyone left in the building at that time, and even Charlie was forced to admit that we had wasted an afternoon.

We travelled home in silence. Charlie was just cold and disappointed, but I felt completely lost. For days I'd been focused on finding the 'mystery person' who seemed to know all about me and my family, and, more strangely still, seemed to care about me so deeply. Now that the search had drawn a blank, life seemed suddenly pointless. The thought of returning to my normal lonely existence – wandering around an empty house, attempting to fill the dragging hours with stupid craze after stupid craze, snatching time with a best friend who was becoming busier and busier by the week – depressed me.

Charlie made one attempt to cheer me up just before he got off the train at the station before mine. 'Don't forget there's the first gala of term this Friday. Psyche yourself up for that – I'm certain you'll get a swim.'

I didn't even look at him, and he jumped off without bothering to say goodbye. He had experienced me in that type of black mood often enough in the past to know there was nothing he could do.

I walked home through the freezing wind without even bothering to put on my coat. I was numb inside and the outside didn't seem to matter. Once in the house I went straight to bed. I lay down and tried to will myself to sleep, but try as I might I couldn't.

Gradually I was filled by a sort of longing; a wistfulness that I couldn't understand. It was like when you wake up feeling happy because you've dreamt something wonderful, but you can't actually remember what the dream was about. I had the sense that now, for the first time, I was about to encounter someone who would transform my life and put it right. Yet I couldn't quite remember who the person was or how I might connect with them.

As I lay on my back in my bed, in a darkened room, in an empty house, I began to cry. I didn't sob or make a single sound, but I could feel the tears building, then sliding out of my eyes and running down my face.

I thought about my parents, who seemed to have no time for me, and I thought about the one person I could have shared all of this with – and I cried even harder because that person, my twin, was dead.

The email had planted in my mind the thought that perhaps there was a God who loved me, but how could I know that such a being existed, and if he did exist how could I reach him?

Still with tears pouring down my face I slipped out of my bed and flicked on the light. I picked up the piece of paper on which I had printed out the email message and I started to read. In 15 minutes I had reached the prayer at the end and I knew what I had to do.

I knelt beside my bed and I began to read, out loud, the prayer that was written down. I asked God to forgive me for everything I could possibly think of, even for still being alive when my beautiful twin sister was dead. I thanked Jesus for dying in my place. And I asked that if he really did love me, would he come into my life and show me he was there?

As I said 'Amen' I started to cry again, but this time it was different. As the tears ran down my cheeks, it seemed to me that my ears popped and my whole world jumped, just a millionth of a millionth of a centimetre, then dropped back into place. Nothing had changed and yet absolutely everything seemed altered. I knelt and I cried – for my sister, for the parents I barely knew, and for myself and my lonely, empty life. As I cried, a warmth seemed to creep up on me and surround me like loving arms. In the end I was crying for the joy of the love and the presence I could feel.

Later I fell asleep, convinced that the barrier had gone and I had met the God who loved me.

Wednesday 31 January, 7.45 am

My alarm clock shattered my peaceful sleep and dragged me into the cold, hard light of day. I remembered immediately what had happened the night before, but the world seemed the same old lonely place again. 'Nothing has changed,' my mind told me. 'You were just tired and emotional last night. What you experienced was nothing more than a pleasant dream.' But I knew it had been real. I knew that something or someone wonderful had touched me, and that when they had been there I had felt different – like a somebody instead of a nobody.

Through the morning I clung desperately to the little warmth and sense of well-being that remained, but even that seemed to dissolve and drift away when confronted by the harsher realities of life at school. No special wonderful presence protected me from humiliation when Phil spent the entire French period making the class laugh at jokes told at my expense. No feeling of well-being encompassed me when he and Sophie walked past me in the hallway and she seemed to turn away in embarrassment, perhaps too ashamed even to admit that she knew me.

That night I walked home through the dark and the cold in confusion. Had something happened or hadn't it? Was God real or wasn't he? If Christianity was worth anything, if God loved me at all, then it had to be true at school, in everyday life, not just in mystical moments late at night.

'Dear . . .? Thank you for your last message – it was very interesting. But I am feeling confused.

'Last night I did as you suggested and I prayed that prayer. If God was real, then I desperately wanted to meet him. At first everything was wonderful. I felt incredible, as though someone who loved me was right there with their arms around me, as though everything was going to turn out all right after all. I really believed that I had somehow become a Christian and that it had changed things.

'But today was different. School was a nightmare and God seemed to have disappeared again. I very nearly decided it had all been a dream, a figment of my imagination, but somehow I just don't know . . .

'Please tell me: how can I be sure that this is all for real?'

Thursday 1 February, 4.00 pm

The return message was waiting for me when I got home from school.

'Dear Dave. What I read today made me very happy. At the very moment you prayed that prayer, you became a new person and received a complete and fresh new start in life.

'As to the rest, don't sweat it! The doubts are entirely normal – everyone experiences them. You were lucky to have the experience of God and his love that you did. I know many people that have been Christians for years who have never had such an amazing experience.

'Here are a few reasons why you can be sure that your new faith is for real.

'First, the Bible. There's just something about food that brings people together. Whether it's a party of five-year-olds with jelly and ice cream, or a pair of lovers making eyes at each other over the spaghetti, friendship and food just seem to go together.

'That's why it is so amazing that in the final book of the Bible (Revelation 3:20) God says that he wants to come into our lives and eat with us. It shows that the relation-ship he wants to have with us is not about religion but about friendship.'

I sat staring into space for some time, absently chewing on a pencil I'd picked up off my desk. Friendship had been in my thoughts a lot lately. With Charlie always so busy, I felt exposed and even lonely. In the past I'd have laughed if someone had suggested to me that God could be part of the solution to my loneliness, but after last night I wasn't laughing any more.

'Have you ever been on holiday to one of the Mediterranean countries where dogs roam the streets? If one takes a liking to you it becomes almost impossible to get rid of. It will follow you across roads, up hills and down steps just because for some reason it has chosen *you*. I wouldn't be so bold as to compare God to a mangy, stray dog but another book of the Bible (Matthew 28:20) says that once God has taken his place in your life he will never leave you.

'Even yesterday at school he was with you, sympathising when you felt down and laughing when you laughed. Just because you couldn't feel him the way you did the night before doesn't change that fact.

'The book of John (20:31) speaks of the eternal life that Jesus promises his followers. This eternal life starts right now and continues beyond the grave. In heaven (a place so wonderful you could break your brain just trying to imagine it) there will be no more crying and no more pain, and there will be no more separation from loved ones. The Bible promises all that to every person who prays as you did the other night and there are many other promises that you could find for yourself if you opened a Bible.'

I got up and went to my bookshelves. Alongside the sci-fi paperbacks and manuals on bird-watching and electronics (yes, they had once been hobbies of mine), there were a few schoolbooks and one Bible. I pulled it down off the shelf and returned to sit at my desk.

The Bible. It had never interested me before but, then again, nor had anything to do with religion. I held it in my hands and fluttered the pages between my fingers. So many pages, so much writing. Where should I start? I considered the beginning, but rejected it. I'd never been the sort of methodical person that reads the instructions or starts at the beginning. I prefer to dive right into something.

That was a big mistake. I opened to a book whose unpronounceable name began with a 'Z' and contained a lot more letters after that. It was a short book, which seemed promising, but things went downhill from there. It was gibberish – to me anyway. All sorts of talk of wrath and anger and judgement – not pleasant reading at all. I tossed the Bible onto my bed in disgust and went back to the email.

'How would you feel if I told you that you had to earn your right to have a relationship with God? Insecure? A little worried?

'Perhaps you'd attempt to impress God? You might be tempted to break the hearts of all the Southerton girls and enter a monastery. You could sell your bike and give the money to the church steeple appeal. You could thrill your parents by inviting the homeless drunk that lives in the centre of town to come and stay at your house.

'Or perhaps, like me, you'd be tempted to give up, certain that however hard you tried you could never make the grade.

'Fortunately it doesn't work like that.

'The event that makes it possible for you to have a relationship with God happened once and for all and in the past, when Jesus died on the cross. The second reason you can be sure about your new faith is because it isn't based on how well you do, but on what Jesus has already done.'

Reading that filled me with genuine relief. My recent experience with the Bible had left me thinking that maybe

I wasn't cut out to be a Christian. If I listened to my mother for long enough it was easy for me to become convinced that I was bound to fail at anything I tried. Even at this early stage I had been starting to wonder if I wouldn't turn out to be a failure as a Christian. Encouraged, I continued to read, not understanding every phrase but excited by the overall message.

'As soon as we start our new relationship with God he comes to live inside us by his Holy Spirit. From that moment on, his presence on the inside begins to change us. It's a bit like putting new software into your computer. The hardware is the same but with a new program inside, the way the computer reacts is different. With God inside you, you are still Dave Johnson, but you might find yourself changing for the better.

'A man called Paul wrote the book of Galatians in the New Testament of the Bible about 2,000 years before the invention of computers, so he had to find another example. He chose fruit. He said that the longer the Holy Spirit lives inside you, the more the fruit grows: gradually love and joy and kindness – the fruits of the Spirit – start to change your relationships with other people . . . and then your whole life. So another way you can be sure of the reality of your relationship with God is if over time you see yourself changing.

'The Holy Spirit inside also helps to convince us that we are loved by God and we are his children. The feeling of love that you had when you first prayed was the Holy Spirit revealing God's heart to you. As more time passes, the Holy Spirit can build in you a certainty of God's love and presence that you can trust even when you can't feel him in that same way.

'I hope, Dave, that all of this helps you to be more confident that what happened to you wasn't just a dream but the beginning of a wonderful new life. Goodbye.'

There were many things about myself that I didn't like, perhaps because my mother was so quick to point my failings out to me. (Maybe that was why I found it so hard to believe Charlie when he told me people liked me.) I had always assumed that I was stuck with my dark moods and my temper, but perhaps now, with God's Spirit living inside me, I could change for the better.

In any case the email had reassured me. I felt confident that what I had experienced was for real. But what now? How did one live as a Christian? How did I communicate with God?

I went back to the Bible, but as hard as I tried to concentrate I noticed my thoughts were turning more and more to the gala that would take place tomorrow. As I wasn't getting anywhere I set about putting my things in order for the big event. We would travel by coach immediately after school, and I didn't want to forget anything. As Charlie had predicted, I had been selected to swim, and although I was only going to be in one relay I intended to give it everything. I now had proper swimming trunks, goggles so I could see where I was going, and flip-flops to wear on the poolside. Charlie had tried to persuade me to buy a swimming cap, but I thought that was going a little too far. I arranged everything in my bag and then settled down for an evening's homework.

Soon the pages in front of me began to blur and I was forced to admit I wasn't going to get anything done that night. I decided it would be better use of my time to email another question to the mystery person. In particular I wanted to know why their view of the Bible (an exciting, wonderful book) and my experience of it (impossible to understand and boring) just didn't seem to match up.

Having sent the message, and given up on homework, I settled down to daydream about the gala. My favourite scenario had me putting in a phenomenally fast relay leg that won the gala for our school. In the ensuing celebrations I could imagine Sophie running over, preferably elbowing Philip Squire aside on her way, throwing her arms around me and giving me a big, passionate, congratulatory kiss. In the background of my daydream all the rest of the team would be applauding me enthusiastically. Then they would carry me out on their shoulders, the conquering hero.

That was the daydream, but the hyperactive butterflies in my stomach reminded me that only tomorrow would tell what would really happen.

Chapter Six

Friday 2 February, 8.10 pm

The evening was not progressing as I had imagined in my daydreams. By the start of the gala I was a nervous wreck. In the half an hour before my race I was having to make frequent trips to the toilet. Five minutes before we were called, I looked so ill that people started asking me if I was going to be sick. Charlie was sitting beside me on the bench at the poolside.

'Don't worry,' he kept repeating over and over again. 'You'll do great. I know you will.'

'But the whole gala will be decided by these last two relays,' I moaned. 'What if I destroy our chances? No one will ever forgive me.'

'Dave, look at me,' said Charlie. I turned my head but even that much movement made me feel seasick. 'This is only a friendly gala; the result doesn't matter. It's just an overgrown practice. Now stop worrying.'

There wasn't much of an audience but all the teams sitting around the poolside were shouting and screaming as the last of the younger age group relays came to an end. In the enclosed and echoing swimming pool the noise was enough to make my head pound.

The tannoy crackled into life as the announcer called the

competitors for my race. I was swimming the breaststroke leg of the senior medley relay: the penultimate race of the night. As the breaststroker I swam second, following Justin swimming backstroke. Then came Phil, who had been switched from breaststroke to fly in order to fit me in and leave a weaker swimmer out. Charlie would swim the anchor leg for us as he was the school's fastest frontcrawler. Since he had done well in the two individual breaststroke events of the gala, finishing second and third, Phil was none too pleased with this arrangement. The coach, however, was insistent. 'This is a team contest,' he said when Philip risked a complaint. 'And I expect you to do what is best for the team, not look for opportunities to show off.'

The look Phil gave me after that little exchange only served to tighten the knots in my stomach.

We all gathered at one end of the pool to receive our instructions. Then, while Phil and Justin took their places at the starter's end of lane five, Charlie and I walked down the poolside to the far end of the lane. Just as we arrived, the backstroke swimmers were called to enter the water and take their starting positions.

The silence terrified me, and as I stood alone on the edge of the pool I felt horribly exposed to the gaze of hundreds of pairs of eyes.

'Take your marks!' shouted the starter.

The only noise was the gentle lapping of the water beneath me. Time seemed to drag. My muscles tightened and I was sure everyone could see me shaking with fear and tension. Finally, the gun went off and Justin flung himself backwards in the water.

He got a good start, but as the eight swimmers moved down the pool towards me he seemed to be losing ground. He was in third place when Charlie started screaming at me to get ready. With my toes curled over the edge of the poolside I stood and shivered, tensed to dive the second Justin touched. Precisely as his hand collided with the end of the pool, I threw myself far out down the centre of the lane.

I fitted in my first stroke while still under water, then came up for breath. I could sense the swimmers on either side and ahead of me, but I refused to be distracted. Instead I focused on long, strong strokes, deep breaths and a fast rhythm. In what seemed like just a few seconds, I was near the end of the pool and needing to judge my line carefully so as to allow Phil room to dive in when I touched. I finished perfectly, just to the edge of the lane, and felt the backwash as Phil hit the water.

By the time I had climbed out and turned to watch, Charlie was on his way back towards me. With excitement I realised we were at least a metre ahead of the field. 'Phil must have swum a great length,' I thought. Then Charlie was home – in first place!

Before the slower teams had even finished, Charlie was shouting at the top of his voice, ignoring the stern looks of the lane judges. 'Dave, that was incredible,' he screamed. 'You gave Phil and me a two-metre head start. And just look at the split time for your length,' he added, pointing to the digital scoreboard. 'It's faster than the winning time for the individual 50 metres breaststroke. Phil won't like that!'

☹ ☹ ☹ ☹ ☹

By then he was out of the pool, and by the time we had walked back to our team area the others had clustered around us. Sophie came up smiling, and while she didn't throw her arms around me and kiss me, or push Phil violently out of the way, her enthusiastic compliments made me grin like an idiot.

We won the gala.

Mr Bishop gathered us all together once we had changed and gave us a little talk on how it had been a good start to the term's competition, but was only the beginning. There was plenty of hard work still to do. To my delight and embarrassment, he even singled me out by name as the best of the new members. Charlie and Sophie smiled warmly, but I remember glancing at Phil and catching a murderous look.

Charlie and I risked the teacher's wrath by running to the corner shop to buy supplies before boarding the coach for the two-hour drive home. Then as we filed down the aisle heading for our usual seats at the back, we saw Sophie sitting alone. Charlie, never one to miss a trick, gave me a huge shove just as I passed, forcing me to drop into the empty seat beside Sophie.

'Well, help yourself, Dave,' she said, sounding cold and offended.

'I'm so sorry. I tripped,' I said as I started to get up.

'Don't worry. I was joking,' she laughed. 'You're more than welcome to sit with me if you'd like to. Nita has deserted me to go and sit with the boys in the back.'

Her grimace told how horrible an experience she felt that would be. I settled down again, not quite sure what to do with myself or what to say. I remained silent and nervous as the coach moved off.

'Are you scared of being driven in coaches?' Sophie asked eventually.

'No,' I replied, genuinely surprised. 'Why?'

'Well, your knuckles are white where you're gripping the armrests.'

I tried to force myself to relax.

'Perhaps I scare you,' said Sophie smiling, as though that was the most unlikely thing in the world.

'Of course it's not that,' I lied. I could scarcely tell her the truth: that I was terrified of her. That I was afraid the closeness, the clean showered smell of her, the occasional touch as our arms brushed, would turn out to be just another of my many daydreams. 'It's just adrenaline from the gala that still has me wound up.'

'You were great,' she said. 'I thought Charlie was just exaggerating when he first told us about you. But as it turns out, he was being uncharacteristically honest.'

The next two hours were heaven for me. As the coach sped along through the night, Sophie and I were in our own small and private world. The other students, the rest of the coach even, seemed to fade away, and not even the loud and obscene songs being sung in the back could break in on us. As we talked, close together in the dark, I began to get to know Sophie as a real person. For the first time she was not just a beautiful stranger about whom I could imagine whatever I wanted, but a real 16-year-old girl with her own problems, hopes and sense of humour.

I realised with a shock that she was someone who could be a friend.

Too soon the coach pulled into the school grounds and parked by the small group of parents sitting in or standing around their cars. I stood up to let Sophie off, and our hands touched, briefly, as we said goodbye.

'See you on Monday, Dave,' said Charlie, shoving past me as he headed off to spend the weekend at someone else's house. 'I hope you enjoyed your journey home,' he called over his shoulder.

As I walked down the road outside the school – no one had come to pick me up – a car swept past and then stopped. The rear window rolled down with a screech of glass on metal, and a head poked out.

'Want a lift, Dave?' Sophie shouted back at me.

The car was already reversing towards me so I didn't really have much choice. I clambered into the back seat beside Sophie.

The drive only took a couple of minutes, but it was long enough for me to start to envy Sophie. Her mum and dad were relaxed and friendly, interested and talkative in a natural way that mine could never quite manage. Laughing at Sophie's commentary on the gala, they enthusiastically complimented me on my swim.

Getting out at the end of my road, I backed away from the car thanking them, possibly a little too profusely, for their kindness. I wasn't aware of the kerb behind me until the back of my right foot hit it. I stumbled backwards, tried to recover, and then, as my other heel snagged on an uneven paving stone, I fell flat on my back.

'Dave!' shouted Sophie, leaning right out of the window and seeming uncertain whether to laugh or not. 'Are you OK?'

'Yes, I'm fine,' I replied a little stiffly.

I cursed myself under my breath for the clumsiness that had spoilt a perfect evening. I stood up and brushed myself off.

'Well, we're off then,' said Sophie's father. Her parents weren't bothering to hide their smiles. 'If you ever need a lift again just ask Sophie.'

Even that wasn't the end of the evening's excitement. My habitual check of my computer revealed an email message. As I didn't have the energy to read a long letter I almost ignored it, but curiosity got the better of me.

'Dave,' the message began, 'why don't we get together so that we can talk more naturally?'

My heart began to beat harder but my shoulders sagged with disappointment as I read on. 'Not face to face of course. As I explained to you once before, I have to keep my identity a secret. I suggest a virtual meeting. Are you registered with ICQ by any chance? Or perhaps another instant messaging service? If so, you can contact me online. I hope you're not planning a hard night's partying because I suggest we meet before 9 am tomorrow – Saturday. I'm afraid I have to be out later.' The mystery person went on to explain the technicalities of where and how I would be able to make contact.

☹ ☹ ☹ ☹ ☹

Saturday 3 February, 7.30 am

In spite of the excitement, I slept the sleep of the exhausted. But towards morning I began to dream disturbing dreams. Vivid images would wake me suddenly and then fade away as I drifted back to sleep. In the pre-dawn hours I had a recurrence of my nightmare.

As usual it began innocently enough. I was floating on a calm sea, under a blue sky, in a little rubber dinghy. At the other end of the dinghy a laughing girl sat facing me: my twin.

With a speed that is only possible in the world of dreams, black clouds raced in from the horizon, quickly covering the sky and plunging us into terrifying darkness. Huge, steep waves swelled up from the previously calm sea and bore down towards us, rushing at us like evil, black-fronted trains.

The dinghy started to buck and toss, more and more wildly, until we were thrown from our seats and forced to cling on to ropes. As the waves got bigger and bigger, we screamed louder and louder, but there was no one to hear us.

One wave rose up bigger and blacker than the rest. It roared towards us and surged under us, lifting us high into the darkness, spinning us upside down, and then flinging us back into the black and swirling sea.

We were under water with vicious currents tearing at us, ripping at us, throwing us this way and that. My twin began to sink into the green darkness, and desperately I reached out for her. Then, just before our fingers entwined, I felt strong hands grab me and I was pulled up, up and away from her.

That was always the end of the nightmare, the point at which I would wake frightened and sweating with the image of my terrified, drowning twin etched in my mind. But that morning the dream continued. For some reason I was able to remember more than usual.

The strong hands continued to drag me up through the water, and then to the surface, out into the light and the air. In my dream, choking and screaming like a baby, I looked up into the face of the young man who had saved me. He was in his mid-teens and he looked hysterical. He was shouting for help and crying at the same time. He rushed up onto the shore and lay me down before dashing back into the sea, still screaming and screaming for help.

Then I woke up.

It was 7.30 am. I climbed out of bed and crept downstairs to the kitchen. As quietly as possible I put the kettle on and made myself a cup of coffee. 'Who was that boy?' I thought to myself. I knew that a teenage boy had dragged me from the sea, but that was all. He saved my life – I ought at least to have been told who he was.

In the past I had raised the question with my parents but had always been met by a wall of stony silence. I resolved to ask again.

By 7.55 am I was logged on to the Net. When I entered my password ICQ informed me that CAT was online. I clicked to contact him, and when a box with flashing cursor appeared I started typing.

'Hi. CAT, R U there?'

For a moment there was no response, and then a line of script began to scroll onto my screen. I felt like a character in a sci-fi film just about to meet face to face with aliens. This was first contact!

'Hey, Dave! Sorry about the hour. I'm afraid Saturdays are a little busy for me right now.'

Just at that moment I was not in the mood for chatting.

'Gr8! But who R U?' I typed.

'Leave it alone, Dave,' came the reply. 'I can't tell you. I have very, very good reasons but you can't possibly know them. Just trust me.'

'How can I trust you? I know nothing about you!!!' I typed, realising that this conversation was too important for texting shortcuts and hoping the exclamation marks would make my point. 'My friend thinks you're a psycho. How do I know you're not?'

It was true – Charlie had all sorts of nasty theories on who might send anonymous communications to 16-year-old boys.

'Dave, it's not like that. You have to believe me. I care about you and want to help you, but I won't tell you any more about myself. Do you want me to continue?'

The screen went blank. I decided to call his bluff and wait him out, but two minutes of silence panicked me. Perhaps he had already gone.

'OK, OK, get on with it,' I typed.

After a few seconds of breathless anxiety, the text began to flow again.

'Thanks, Dave. Now let's get back to the Bible. You

seem to have had trouble reading it, or even understanding what is so special about it. Am I right?'

'Well, yes,' I replied. 'Not 2 b rude but 2 me it's just a confusing old book with nothing to say.'

'Well, I don't mean 2 b rude either,' came the reply, copying my texting shortcuts for once but still typing so quickly that it was clear they weren't needed, 'but you seem to be forgetting that the Bible is the world's number one bestseller – 4.4 million sold every year! Forget horror or romance, the Bible outsells them all. It must have something to say.'

'But I'm a teenager in the 21c. What can such an old book tell me?'

'Much more than you seem to think. OK, the Bible was written thousands of years ago by men that wouldn't have known what a television was if it jumped up and bit them. But those men were guided and directed by God himself. The Bible is God's book and because he is the creator of all life it can be seen as a manual for life, even life in the twenty-first century.

'I don't know if you've ever done the Boy Scout thing – night hikes, orienteering and walks in the woods. If you have tried the outdoor life you might know the difference between a compass and a map, and you might understand why the Bible is more like a compass. You see, a compass can't show you every twist and turn of a route – it can't tell you that Farmer Giles's farm is to the left and that the local Happy Eater is to the right – but it is essential for not getting lost. A compass gives you a bearing on where you are and where you should go.

'The Bible is the same. It can't tell us what to do in every situation – there's no commandment saying, "Thou shalt not watch MTV because the presenters use rude words" – but it does tell us how we should live in order to please God. It also promises that if we live in that way, we will be making the most of our lives. Christians who choose to follow God's instructions in the Bible, find it actually leads to more freedom and a better life.'

I sat at my desk and pondered what had just been said. I understood the argument but it was still a bit cold; a bit like a set of instructions left by a distant disciplinarian father.

'I see wot u r saying,' I typed, almost thinking aloud. 'But a manual for living doesn't match up with all that u told me about God's luv.'

'You're right! As well as a guide for life, the Bible is also like a personal letter from God to you. All relationships involve communication, and the number one way that God speaks to us is through the Bible.

'Look, I'm really sorry, Dave, but I've got to go soon. Maybe we can meet like this again?'

'Sounds gr8!' I replied. 'But wot if I wanna read the Bible? Wot do I need to do to understand it and hear from God? Where should I start? Wot shd I read?'

'If I were you I would start reading one of the Gospels, the stories of Jesus' life, either Matthew, Mark, Luke or John. Why not try to read a little bit of the Bible every day – not so much that you get bored, just a few minutes' worth? Choose a quiet place where you won't be disturbed, at a time when you're not too rushed. First pray and ask God to speak to you by his Spirit through the Bible, then start reading. As you read don't just let your mind shut down. Keep asking yourself, "What does this say?" "What does this mean?" "What does it mean to me?" There are even Bible-reading notes specially written for young people to help you get to grips with these questions. If you're still struggling I could probably get hold of some for you.

'Whatever you do just keep going.'

After that we said our goodbyes and arranged to meet at the same time and place next week. As I lay back down, intending to spend a lazy Saturday morning watching TV in bed, two mysteries occupied my mind. I solemnly swore to myself that I would find out more about the details of the drowning tragedy, and that one way or another I would find out who this mystery Christian was.

Chapter Seven

Tuesday 6 February, 1.00 pm

By Tuesday it was obvious that I had been promoted to a higher level on the school social pyramid. Being seen around with Charlie had always helped my social standing, but even his patronage had never drawn me into the 'in crowd'. In the past they had tolerated me when he was around; after all there was nothing really weird about me – I didn't wear horrible clothes or listen to hideous music. But they ignored me when I was on my own.

Now that had changed. It must have had something to do with the increased amount of time I spent with Sophie, and the rather embellished reports of my role in the school's gala victory that Charlie had spread around.

That lunchtime Sophie, Charlie and I were sitting in the cafeteria toasting each other with plastic cups of water. We had just survived a double French lesson during which, in an all-too-common moment of boredom, Charlie had calculated that we had only 25 more to endure before our GCSEs.

As we sat and laughed, Justin wandered over. He sauntered up and sat down in the way of someone who has a specific purpose but wants to look as if he's just passing the time.

'What have you three spiked your drinks with?' he asked. 'Nobody has that much fun on water.'

'I'll tell you, if you promise not to tell Phil,' said Charlie with a subtle nod to the table where Phil was sitting. (Phil was a prefect of course.)

'Is there really something in it then?' Justin's eyes widened. (He was a good swimmer but not too bright.)

'Of course not, Justin,' said Sophie. She was too kind-hearted to watch anyone being strung along. 'Charlie's joking. Now tell us what you want.'

'Nothing,' said Justin. 'I was just wandering by on my way out.'

'Yeah right,' said Charlie. 'After five years at this school, even you couldn't get lost in the cafeteria, and the exit is that way.' He pointed. 'Now, as the nice lady said, tell us what you want.'

'OK then,' said Justin. 'It's no big deal. I know you two can't make it, but I wanted to ask Dave to my party on Saturday night.'

That threw me. The parties that Justin and his brother gave were famous, but not for reasons that made me anxious to be there. They were notorious for the amount of alcohol consumed, for the amount of damage caused and for the frequency with which the police were the last in a long line of gatecrashers.

'Um, well thanks, Justin,' I muttered. 'That's a really kind offer, but . . . well . . . I already have plans for Saturday night . . . I think.'

'No sweat,' said Justin. 'Just wanted you to know you were welcome.'

'I hope I didn't offend him,' I said as soon as Justin was out of earshot.

'Don't worry about it,' said Charlie. 'You should hear what his parents called him when they saw the state of their house after his last party. Now that was offensive!'

'Have you really got plans for Saturday?' asked Sophie.

'No,' I replied.

'Good, because I wanted to give you this.'

She pulled a white envelope out of her bag and handed it to me. Inside was a simple white card embossed with gold lettering. 'You are invited to the sixteenth birthday celebration of Sophie Tanner,' it read. 'Please arrive at the Belle Epoch restaurant in smart dress at 7.45 pm on Saturday 10 February.'

'I'm sorry it's such short notice, Dave. Can you make it?' asked Sophie.

'Of course he can,' Charlie answered for me. 'In all the years I've known Dave, the only time he's had plans for Saturday night was when he had an operation scheduled to remove his appendix.'

'I'd love to come. Thank you,' I cut in over Charlie.

'That's great,' said Sophie. 'I'll see you there. I've got to go now – homework to finish for this afternoon.'

'Dave, you are home and dry with that girl,' said Charlie. 'I don't know what she sees in you, but I know that she had to go to a lot of trouble to get you that invitation at the last minute – the rest were distributed ages ago. If you don't take your chance with her,' continued Charlie, 'I will never forgive you.'

Wednesday 7 February, 8.00 pm

It was a week of birthdays, and Wednesday 7 February was my father's. Each year we 'celebrated' (if I can use that word for such a dull, lifeless occasion) with a family meal at home. Invariably it was a time of embarrassment, struggling and dying conversations, and long silences. You simply can't live separate lives and then try to be a happy family a few times a year.

For once, though, I was looking forward to the event. I was high on the euphoria of my school experiences and Sophie's invitation, and I wanted to quiz my parents about the boy who had saved my life. I was too keyed-up to consider that it wasn't really an appropriate subject matter for a birthday party, or to contemplate that they might not want to talk about it.

The meal began as family tradition dictated, with my father's favourite homemade vegetable soup. 'This is wonderful, darling,' said my father, keeping to the safe script for such occasions.

He spooned in another mouthful and I studied him as he ate. He is much older than my mother, twelve years in fact, and that day was his 57th birthday. My father is, above all else, a businessman and he looks and dresses like one. He spends far more time at the office doing deals for his company than he spends at home with us.

I have never felt close to him; in fact I scarcely know him, and I doubt that my mother and he have much of a relationship any more. I suppose they must have loved each other once – I mean, my twin and I arrived by the usual methods – but for as long as I can remember they have spent no more time together than is absolutely necessary. When he speaks to me, particularly on special occasions, it is with the kind of false friendliness normally reserved for young second cousins and other distant relations.

'How is life for you then, Dave-my-boy?' he began, once the soup had been cleared away. 'Your mother tells me that you've taken up diving or something.'

'Actually it's swimming,' I corrected him half-heartedly.

'I hope that it's not interfering with your "O" levels.'

'They're called GCSEs now,' said my mother. She had returned with the main course: lamb cutlets were another of my father's favourites.

'Well, whatever,' he continued, unabashed. 'Just remember that schoolwork must have the top priority. Swimming coach is not exactly the kind of job your mother and I have in mind for you.'

I bit down hard on my lamb, determined not to lose my temper. It always infuriated me that my father could ignore me 99 per cent of the time and then, on the few occasions we actually spoke, treat me like a six-year-old in need of his guidance just to tie my shoelaces. Instead of screaming with frustration I tried to steer the conversation towards my rescuer.

'I was thinking about our old house the other day,' I began. 'Wasn't it right by the sea . . .'

'Please let's not talk about the past,' said my mother quickly. 'We're trying to celebrate.'

'Nonsense,' said my father. 'There's no harm in talking

about the old place. It's my birthday and it was my family home after all. What did you want to know about it?'

'I was just wondering why we moved from such a wonderful place to a dump like Southerton,' I said.

My mother started to protest, but my father kept on.

'We moved because of the accident, Dave. After your sister's death it was simply too painful to stay there. We wanted a fresh start where we could forget all about the past, and Southerton was convenient for my job.'

I saw that my mother was about to change the subject, so I plunged ahead.

'Who was the boy that rescued me on the day of the accident?'

There was silence around the table. I watched my parents carefully, hoping to learn from their responses. My mother stole a quick, nervous glance at my father and in the seconds that followed his face paled and a tremor momentarily shook his hands. I was surprised; normally nothing bothered my father.

'Look, David,' said my mother. 'We've been over that ground in the past and we told you then that it was a very brave passer-by we have never seen before or since. Please forget about it.'

'You must know something,' I protested. 'He saved my life!'

I had pushed too far. My father exploded.

'You selfish boy! This is my birthday and you seem determined to spoil it with painful memories. Get out! Be so kind as to leave us to finish our meal in peace.'

I stood to my feet. By now I too was angry.

'Did it ever occur to you that I might have painful memories too?' I spoke as slowly and calmly as I could. 'And it only makes things worse when you seem to be hiding something from me. I intend to find out what you're lying about and why!'

I stood up and stormed out.

Thursday 8 February, 3.50 pm

After school I rushed straight home and shut myself in my parents' office, confident that I had plenty of time before either of them returned. It was a small room looking out onto the back garden. As well as an office it was also the storeroom for all of our family documents. Most of these were kept in a battered old filing cabinet.

I slipped the catch and pulled the top drawer open. Inside were hanging files, carefully labelled and neatly arranged by my meticulous mother. I pulled out two: one was mine and the other – a much thinner one – had my sister's name written along the spine.

Over the years I had often crept into this room to get at these files, to look at pictures of my sister and to read the reports from health officials and nursery workers that told me all I knew about her and her short life.

One favourite photo showed the whole family sitting together on a rug in an isolated field. The look of pleasure and happiness on my parents' faces, and the natural way in which my sister and I were holding each other, told of a love and togetherness that our family had not known since her death.

I studied this picture again, wondering for the first time who my parents could have found to take a photo in such a deserted place. Perhaps it had been done on a timer?

The final sheet of paper in the file was my sister's death certificate. Many times in the past I had cried as I read the stark details of an event that had changed my life. Of course, I found nothing new. Quickly I thumbed through my own file, and then even through those belonging to my parents, but I found nothing else of interest, and nothing about the accident.

That left only the safe to try.

The safe was a black, steel box that stood alone in one corner of the office. The combination was simple and I had discovered it years ago during a childish craze for spying. I opened the thick, heavy door and carefully read through the labels on another set of hanging files. Mostly they were bank or company names; a few were labelled more personally, probably business contacts of my mother's; but one stood out. It said, simply, 'Christopher'. This was the file I took out. It was thick with papers, so I retreated to a chair to read it.

As I crossed the room, a photo fell from the file to the floor, and I stooped to pick it up. The photo was almost identical to the one I had studied a few minutes earlier, but there was one striking difference. My father had disappeared, presumably he was behind the camera, and in his place sat a teenage boy. My twin and I were bouncing on his knees, still holding hands and laughing hilariously. I looked more closely at the smiling boy. His was the face I had seen in my nightmare! But who was he?

I stuffed the picture into my pocket, sunk into a chair and opened the file. A birth certificate: 'Christopher Anthony Johnson. Born 3rd April to Mr Arthur Dennis Johnson and Mrs Penelope Anne Johnson.' That was my father's name, but I didn't recognise the woman's – it certainly wasn't my mother. So what did that make Christopher? My half-brother? If I had a brother then where was he? Surely he hadn't died too. I shuffled through the file, quickly passing school reports, medical records and more photos. Near the back of the file I found a sheet of newspaper, folded and yellowed with age. Under the bold headline, 'Twin Dies in Drowning Tragedy', I read the following:

> Tragedy struck our tranquil community last week when the two-year-old daughter of Mr and Mrs Arthur Johnson fell from the dinghy in which she and her twin brother were playing and drowned in the sea. What were two two-year-olds doing playing alone in a dinghy in the sea? At the time of the accident the twins were in the care of their older half-brother, Christopher Johnson. While he was down the beach purchasing ice creams, his baby brother and sister were drowning.
>
> Christopher Johnson maintains that he left the twins pulled high up on the beach, and that only a wave of freak size could possibly have reached and re-floated them. When he returned and found the twins in trouble, he plunged into the sea and managed to save one twin, the boy. Some time later, the small lifeless body of the girl was also recovered by the police.

> This newspaper has it on good authority that taking the twins to the beach in the first place was against the wishes of Mr and Mrs Johnson. While no criminal charges have been laid against Master Johnson as of yet, we can surely state that this is not the last word on this terrible tragedy. Rest assured, you will be able to read about any future developments right here in the *Chronicle*.

What I had discovered blew my mind. I had a half-brother who was, at least in part, responsible for my sister's death – and also responsible for saving my life. Somehow he had disappeared, and my parents refused even to admit his existence. What had happened to him?

I checked the date on the birth certificate. By my calculations he would have been 16 when the accident occurred and, if he was still alive, he would be 29 now.

I pulled the photo out of my pocket and stared at it once more. So where was he?

Saturday 10 February, 8.15 am

I was sitting bleary-eyed, with a steaming cup of coffee beside me, in front of my computer. I had skipped Friday's swimming practice because after my discovery of a half-brother I had felt in need of time to think. In spite of an early night I had not slept well.

'Morning, Dave!'

'Hi,' I replied, unable to persuade my sleepy fingers to type more than two letters.

'How has the Bible reading been going then?'

'Better,' I admitted.

'In that case I think it's time for us to talk about prayer. What do you know about that?'

'Not much,' I replied. 'But I think I could probably stumble my way through the "Our Father".'

'That's great, but prayer is more than just finding a beautiful prayer and then reading it back to God.

'Think what it would be like if someone decided that they would only communicate with their girlfriend by reading her poetry. Romantic moments below the stars would be blissful – what better way to win a girl's heart? She would swoon to the words of Shakespeare's Sonnets and fall into her Romeo's arms. But very soon the relationship would stop growing and start stagnating.

'It's very hard to find a poem that says, "I love you but I've had a bad day and I need to be alone." It's even harder to find one that accurately communicates, "I'll meet you at the bus stop at 6.15," or, "I'm having a burger and fries – would you like the onion rings?"

'In relationships, we need to be able to speak from the heart about the things that matter to us right at that moment. It's the same with prayer. Prayer is about a relationship with God, and it's hard to have a decent relationship with him if you can only communicate using pre-prepared speeches. It would make it impossible to share with him what is going on in your life or to tell him how you are feeling, and your friendship with him would stop growing.

'Think of prayer as talking with God – there are no rules,

you are free to use whatever words you choose. As time goes by it will get easier and you'll feel able to tell him everything.'

I took another gulp of coffee and let the caffeine and the prayer information filter into my sleep-clouded mind together.

'But I always thought prayer was about asking God for things?'

'No, not really – it's best to think of it as a relationship. Having said that, when you pray you are speaking to the Creator of the universe, the most powerful being in existence, so it'd be odd not to ask him for his help once in a while. After all, there is no prayer he can't answer, and as our loving Father he wants to help us.'

'Not all prayers are answered, though,' I protested. 'I've prayed in the past and absolutely nothing has happened. Why was that?'

'Well, think what a disaster it would be if a parent decided that they would give their child absolutely whatever they asked for. You can imagine the toddler playing in the corner with the nice, shiny carving knife, or the six-year-old proudly showing off his loaded magnum revolver to his friends. It would be an outrage, and everyone would shout and scream about how irresponsible the parent was.

'Parents are expected to know better than their children what is good for them. In the same way, God often knows what we need better than we do. When we are selfish or foolish he sometimes gives us what we need in place of what we ask for.'

Suddenly, and for no apparent reason, things clicked. It was as though there had been two great seas of thought locked up in my head, but kept separate in their own compartments. Now, suddenly, the dam broke and the two rushed together and mixed in a flash of comprehension that set my mind alight.

Of course! How could I not have seen it before? The mystery person and my lost half-brother Christopher – they had to be one and the same! It explained everything. He knew me, but I didn't know him. He knew about my family. And his log-on name CAT was composed of his initials, if he had changed his last name to something beginning with T. Christopher Anthony T . . .

Only when the screen saver appeared on my computer monitor did I realise that I must have been sitting thinking for some minutes. The mystery person (my half-brother?) was obviously expecting some comment from me. I willed my brain back onto the subject of prayer. I didn't want to break this contact, but I needed some time before I made my thoughts public.

'I've just been thinking,' I typed. 'And what you've said makes a lot of sense to me, but could you please give me some practical advice on how to pray? Something like the practical advice you gave me on reading the Bible.'

I ignored the answer as it scrolled onto my screen. Time was of the essence now. What should I do? How would he respond if I confronted him with what I thought? What if I was wrong?

One thing was clear to me. If he had gone to all this trouble to speak to me in a completely anonymous way, then it must be very important to him that my parents didn't know who he was, or that he was in contact with me. That, combined with the fact that I knew where he worked, should provide some leverage.

As his answer ended I prepared to drop my bombshell.

'I know who you are. If you refuse to talk to me honestly about your identity then I will tell my parents all I know, which includes your name and the fact that you work for Creative Software Designs of 122 Woolson Street.

'You are Christopher Anthony Johnson and you are my half-brother.'

Nothing happened. I sat with the tension tying knots in the muscles of my neck and shoulders as seconds built into minutes. Finally it was too much.

'Speak to me,' I typed. Still nothing happened. I tried a bit more pressure. 'My mother is downstairs right now. Should I go and tell her about you?'

Finally script started scrolling onto my screen.

'No, Dave, please don't do that. Perhaps that time will come, but not yet.'

'I want to meet you,' I typed.

'I don't think that's a very good idea. You shouldn't arrange meetings with people you don't know.'

'Don't know! You're my half-brother. You saved my life. You told me about God. I can bring your birth certificate with me if you want. I have a picture of you in my hand right now. Of course I know you. Meet me . . . today!'

There was another long pause, but then one last line of script appeared on the screen.

'OK, you win. Central Station at 7.00 pm tonight. Don't worry. I'll recognise you.'

A system message appeared stating that the connection had been broken.

I tilted back in my chair, still trying to comprehend what was happening. Tonight I would be coming face to face with the mystery person, and also with a half-brother I never even knew I had.

Another thought hit me: Sophie's party!

Chapter Eight

Saturday 10 February, 6.00 pm

'This can't be happening to me!' I slammed the phone back down and kicked the side of the phone box in frustration. 'Where is he?'

I had been trying to contact Charlie all day, and not once had he or his mother been home. To make matters worse, they didn't have an answer machine and whenever I rang Charlie's mobile I got a message telling me, 'This unit is no longer taking incoming calls.' Why did they both have to hate technology so much? Now it was 6.02. I was at Southerton Station and my train was due to leave in less than five minutes. I was desperate to speak to Charlie so that he could explain to Sophie why I was not going to be at her party.

From the moment the message had appeared on my screen I had done nothing but worry over where I should be at 7.00 that evening. Everything in me wanted to be with Sophie, but bad as I felt about letting her down, and worried though I was about who might make a move on her in my absence, I had finally decided that I must meet my brother.

Still standing in the phone box, much to the annoyance of the queue waiting outside, I looked at my watch. My train would leave in three minutes. With a horrible sinking feeling I resigned myself to the inevitable. I couldn't contact Charlie and I had no other way of getting a message to Sophie – she had never given me her number and I didn't know her address. I wondered whether she would ever speak to me again. Well, so be it. I clenched my jaw and tried to pull myself together. This meeting with my brother was not something I could just walk away from. I set out at a run for platform four.

After searching through three carriages I finally found an empty seat and settled down for the journey. I had already decided that the 40 minutes between Southerton and the city centre would be a good opportunity to try this 'prayer' thing – I was that desperate.

I pulled a folded piece of paper out of my pocket and re-read the mystery person's, or rather my brother's, advice.

'Like reading the Bible, prayer is easiest when you are alone and do not have too much on your mind.'

'Great!' I thought, looking around the crowded carriage. I carried on reading.

'If you're stuck about how to begin, try using this pattern: first, thank God for all that he has given you. Second, say sorry for anything you have done wrong. Ask him to forgive you and to help you to change. Finally, feel free to ask for his help in areas that you, or those you care about, need it.'

I read and re-read the piece of paper, but I simply couldn't concentrate. By the time I arrived at the end of a sentence, I'd already forgotten what the first half had been talking about. It was no use. Patterns for praying would have to come later. For now it was all I could do to murmur, over and over, 'Please God, let it all be OK!' It seemed to work; as I prayed I began to feel more confident.

Eventually the train slowed for the final time and we slipped in under the vast roof of Central Station.

I waited in my seat as the other passengers swept off the train. Once the carriage was empty I stood up and self-consciously rearranged my crumpled clothes, tucking a loose scrap of shirt back into my jeans, and then checked my appearance in the small stainless steel mirror beside the door. I wanted to make a good impression.

As I walked down the platform, past the ticket collector and out into the huge, high-ceilinged concourse, I was swallowed up into the crowd of thousands of Saturday-night revellers. I doubted that I would ever find my brother in this chaos.

For a while I stood bewildered and disorientated as people swirled past me, but after a few minutes the dizzi-ness passed and I began to pick out the scattered individ-uals and small groups who were not moving with the crowds. Over there, an air stewardess, holding a small overnight case and probably waiting for a train to the airport. A little to my right, a group of girls, laughing and joking as they passed around a large bottle of cheap spirits. Standing just a few feet from me and scanning the crowds, a menacing looking man in a long black overcoat. A young guy in a leather jacket passed by me a number of times, obviously looking for someone. I pulled the now crumpled photo of my half-brother from my pocket and studied it carefully, wondering if possibly . . . but the next time I saw the guy in the leather jacket he had his arms around a very pretty girl and I got the impression he wasn't looking for anyone else.

The longer I waited the more tense I became. I was worried that my brother might not turn up, and scared of what would happen if he did. What would he be like? What if I didn't like him? Worse still, what if he didn't like me? My nervousness played tricks on my mind and I fell prey to sudden, senseless cravings. For a minute I desperately wanted a cigarette, even though I had never smoked. Next I was tempted to go and ask the group of girls for a swig from their bottle, yet I almost never drank. Finally I settled on chewing my nails. Moments later, disgusted with myself, I spat the little slivers of nail onto the concrete floor and looked for other ways to distract myself. I studied the air stewardess, trying to guess from the colours of her uniform which airline she worked for, and wondering where in the world she was headed. Something happened as I watched. One moment she was standing there slumped and bored and the next she was alert and poised. It was as if a waxwork figure had come to life.

I searched around for what had triggered the transformation and finally I found it, or rather I found him. A tall man was walking straight towards the stewardess. He might have been very good-looking (I'm no expert when it comes to good-looking men), or it might have been the confidence he exuded, but something about him had certainly caught her attention. I watched with interest as he walked up to the air stewardess, and I sensed her disappointment as he walked straight past. It wasn't until he stopped in front of me and spoke my name that I even considered he might be approaching me.

He tried my name again, and this time he reached out his hand. I responded by reflex and returned his handshake. Time seemed to stop still.

'Idiot,' I thought to myself. Subconsciously I had been expecting a 16-year-old boy like the one in the photo, like me, and I had not considered the change 13 years or more would make.

'Dave?'

'Christopher?' I replied, my voice shaky and too quiet in the noisy station.

'That's me,' he said. 'It's great to see you. Incredible really.' He paused as though expecting me to speak, but words simply weren't forming themselves in my mind and I stood there blankly until he continued. 'Have you eaten?' he said. I shook my head, still mute. 'Good. I know a restaurant about a five-minute walk from here. I'll buy you something to eat and we can talk.'

Even as he spoke, he started to walk towards one of the exits, and I fell numbly into step beside him. About 50 paces later I stopped suddenly and once again pulled the photo from my pocket. Christopher also stopped, and as he turned back towards me I raised the photo and compared the face in the picture with the man who stood before me. There had been a number of stories in the news recently about adults luring young people to secret meetings by lying about their identity on the Internet and in chatrooms. While I was 99 per cent sure I was not being tricked (after all, it was I who had tracked Christopher and pressured him into this meeting), I was also painfully aware that nobody, not even Charlie, knew where I was at that moment.

I looked the stranger up and down and compared the old photo with the present reality. While there was no distinctive family likeness, there was nothing to make it hard to believe he was my half-brother, and the boy in the photo and the man who stood before me were definitely the same person.

'Just checking,' I muttered under my breath, and started walking again.

'Was your journey OK?' Christopher asked moments later. I imagine he was starting to wonder if I was capable of conversation, but he ploughed on anyway. 'I guess all of this is more of a shock for you than for me. I've known who I was talking to all along, whereas you've only just found out. And by the way, I'd like to know how you did find out.'

To my immense relief he chatted freely as we left the station and walked down a busy road.

'Here's the place.' We had turned down a narrow side street, and he pushed open the door to a small restaurant.

'Table for two,' he told the waiter who had been hovering by the door.

We were led past the few other early customers to a table placed in a secluded corner.

To my great relief, Chris was talkative and funny, and

eventually I relaxed. He seemed content just to chat and joke, but beneath what I hoped was a calm exterior my questions were boiling over. In the end, it was all too much.

'Forty-eight hours ago I didn't even know you existed,' I blurted out. 'How about an explanation?'

Chris seemed shocked. 'You never knew about me?' he asked.

'No. Never. Nothing,' I replied.

'And you don't remember me? I suppose you wouldn't,' he continued, speaking almost to himself. 'You were only two when the accident happened, and then, what with the move to Southerton and everything, I guess there would have been nothing to remind you.'

He took on a thoughtful expression and we sat in silence for some moments. Eventually he continued. 'I always assumed that you knew about me but just didn't care,' he said. 'Or hated me because of what happened. Do you hate me?' he asked with a sudden look of anguish on his face.

'No, I don't hate you. I don't even know you,' I replied. 'But I'm confused and you're going to have to tell me the whole story, right from the beginning.'

And that's what he did for the next hour-and-a-half. Through the salad starter, and the main course, right up until pudding. It was not a pretty story.

My father's first marriage had ended in a bitter divorce, with Chris's mother fleeing the country and heading back to her family in Canada, leaving no forwarding address. As if his real mother's desertion wasn't bad enough, the second marriage landed Chris with a cold and uninterested stepmother. The birth of twins – my sister and I – had brightened things for a time, but then real tragedy struck.

To retell the events of that day was obviously still painful and even physically difficult for Chris. He stared over my shoulder, refusing to meet my eyes and speaking flatly, like a bored student reading an English essay. Eventually his voice cracked, and he had to pause for a minute. Starting again, he told of how a policeman had had to physically drag him from the sea when it was decided that the search for my sister was useless.

'I'm certain it wasn't your fault,' I said, but the words sounded empty, even to me.

Chris continued with the story.

After the accident my mother held him responsible, and swore that she would never forgive him. My father, grief-stricken and confused himself, could do nothing to help mend the situation. In the end, with nowhere else to turn, and almost drowning in his guilt, Chris had run away to the city and had not spoken to my parents since.

As pudding was served, Chris's story raised new questions in my mind.

'But that was 13 years ago. Did you never try to make contact?' I asked.

'For the first year or more I was determined not to contact them,' said Chris. 'I didn't want their help and I was too angry to even phone and tell them I was OK. Then, when I did return, I got the shock of my life. The house was empty. I had been abandoned! I was so hurt and so angry that I came back here and swore I'd make it on my own and never look for them again.'

By now the restaurant had become busy and every table was occupied. When, for the third time in ten minutes, the waiter appeared asking if there was anything else we needed, Chris took the hint. He paid up and we left.

Back out in the cold we wandered towards the station.

'Perhaps you ought to get back,' said Chris, looking at his watch.

For the first time my mind flickered back to Sophie, Charlie and the party. I extended my arm to look at my own watch. It was already 9.00 pm. There was no hope of my making it to the restaurant now.

'I'm in no hurry,' I said. 'There's a lot more I still want to hear.'

'Join me for another coffee,' said Chris, 'and I'll tell you the rest.'

He stepped into the road and shouted to catch the attention of a passing taxi.

'It's too cold for walking the streets,' he said. 'We'll take a taxi and I'll take you to one of my favourite places.'

Ten minutes later we arrived outside a run-down coffee shop. Almost before he had crossed the threshold Chris was calling out to the elderly man behind the counter.

'Two of your finest coffees, Tony!'

We sat down at a small, coffee-stained, plastic table.

'Tony would hate me to tell you,' said Chris, 'but I owe him a lot. When I first ran away he used to let me do odd jobs for him in return for food – he probably kept me from starving to death. He was also the one who took me along to meet the people who run "Lifelines". It's a Christian hostel for young people,' he explained. 'They took me in, helped me get my life sorted out, and eventually found a place for me on a computer studies course at a technical college. Much later I became a Christian.'

'But how did you find us?' I asked. 'Why get in contact now after so many years? Tell me everything.'

'Well,' Chris began, 'for years, maybe a whole decade, I hated Dad and hated my stepmother – your mother – even more. It's scary to look back because I wonder what I would have done if I had somehow bumped into them in the street. I honestly wanted to kill them.'

'So what changed?' I asked.

'I guess I did,' replied Chris. 'It took a long time, but after I became a Christian I gradually began to see that it's not good to carry a lot of hatred and hurt around. Looking back it's almost as if God has been guiding me towards reconciliation for years.

'First he used the Bible. As I read that book more and more I realised that my attitudes were wrong.'

'No they weren't,' I burst out. 'You had every right to hate them. I can't believe how badly they treated you!'

'Certainly I had reason to feel the way I did,' admitted Chris. 'But the Bible is very clear in teaching that we must forgive people, even when they hurt us.'

Tony chose that moment to bring two huge pastries to our table. I was still full from our meal, but they did look good and, as Tony put it, they were 'Gratis, on the house'.

Chris teased him about his generosity which meant that

the little business never made a profit, but Tony only laughed and left us to continue our conversation.

'Forgiving them was only the start though,' said Chris. 'Over the months and years there grew an almost overwhelming desire to see you all again. I turned to friends at my church for advice. Unfortunately, while they were very caring and supportive, they couldn't tell me what I should do. They simply told me to keep on praying and to use my commonsense. That's what I did. I prayed and I did some very simple detective work. I was certain that if Dad was anywhere in this part of the country he would still be working for his old company. So I started hanging around outside their office buildings at the end of the working day and, sure enough, one evening I spotted Dad and simply followed him home to Southerton. At that point I didn't know what to do. Suddenly all my dreams were possible. I could simply walk up, knock on the door and that would be it.'

'So, why didn't you?' I asked.

'I was too scared,' replied Chris. 'I still am. I had no idea what they would say if they saw me. They could so easily reject me again, and I'm not sure that I could stand that. I'm afraid that's the real reason I invited you to meet me here, in the city. As much as I dream about seeing Dad again, I am also terrified by the thought. Knowing where you all were and yet not knowing what to do was horrible. I would often drive or take the train down to Southerton and sit looking at the house, thinking of you all and praying. Sometimes I would see you coming out, and I'm embarrassed to admit that on occasions I even followed you.'

My surprise must have shown on my face because Chris hurried to explain himself.

'I know it sounds really weird, but you have to try to understand how I felt. I really wanted to speak to you, to tell you who I was, but I just couldn't drum up the courage to do it, and so I ended up just following you around. Can you forgive me for that?'

'Of course,' I said. 'There's nothing to forgive. Tell me what happened next.'

'The more I prayed, the more convinced I became that God wanted me to contact you and that he wanted me to tell you about Christianity. I knew there was no better gift I could give you than the knowledge that you could have a relationship with God. I just knew that was what God was saying to me.'

'Saying to you?' I asked. 'You heard him speak?'

'Nothing audible,' said Chris. 'No deep voice shaking the walls and waking the neighbours – just a conviction of what God wanted me to do. Don't look so shocked,' he laughed. 'The Bible promises Christians can grow to recognise God's voice and be guided by him in their lives.'

My thoughts turned once again to Sophie and her birthday party. An image sprang into my mind of all the guests seated around a table. I knew that no matter how many conversations were going on, I would be able to hear Sophie's voice above everyone else's. It wasn't that her voice was loud, it was just that I had trained my ear to pick hers out. I supposed that some people could recognise God's voice in the same way.

Chris continued. 'As I prayed about how I should

contact you, God continued to guide me, but this time through a most amazing coincidence. A couple of friends approached me to ask if I would be willing to use my computer programming skills to work with them on putting together an introduction to the Christian faith on CD ROM. I loved the idea and we all started work immediately.

'It was then that everything clicked into place. I knew how I could make an initial contact and speak to you about Christianity at the same time. Even better, I could do it all without having to risk meeting you or being discovered by your parents.

'That was a year ago now. It took us that long to develop the software and for me to create the specially personalised version that I posted to you a few weeks ago. When it came to it, my resolve deserted me and I couldn't bear to just send it off and forget about it. That was when I incorporated the secret message at the end that gave you my email address. I must admit, though, I didn't bargain on your being able to track me down. You must tell me how you managed that.'

I told Chris my side of the story, about Natasha tracing the email address and my trip with Charlie to Creative Software Designs. When I came to the part about seeing him in my dream, Chris interrupted me.

'It sounds as if God was guiding you too.' I looked blankly at him. 'You see God sometimes uses dreams to guide his people,' explained Chris. 'Admittedly using a nightmare seems unusual, but I have no doubt that God's hand was in the sudden recovery of your memory that led to your seeing my face in that dream.'

That gave me something to think about, but I decided that I liked the idea that God's hand was on me. When I had finished the story I reluctantly decided that it was time for me to go. My first meeting with Chris had gone better than I could possibly have hoped, so when he asked if I wanted to see him again I jumped at the chance. In fact we agreed to meet the very next day.

I reached home just before midnight and was surprised to see lights still on downstairs.

'Where have you been?' demanded my mother as she met me at the door. 'Your father and I have been worried sick about you. Charlie has phoned at least five times asking where you are, insisting that something must have happened to you. He kept going on about some party that he knew you would never miss. So where have you been?'

'Just walking,' I replied. I still had no qualms about lying to protect my secret.

'I don't believe that,' said my mother. 'Charlie insisted that nothing would make you miss this party.'

'Look, I just didn't feel like it, all right? You and Charlie can think what you want, but it's my life.'

'Well, that's fine by me,' said my mother, already bored of the conversation now that she knew nothing serious had happened to me. 'But you'll have to explain to Charlie. He said he'd wait by the phone until we had news of you. You'd better ring him right now.'

Chapter Nine

Sunday 11 February, 12.15 am

The late night phone conversation with Charlie was going downhill fast. To begin with he had been full of concern, but now that he knew I hadn't gone under a bus he was livid.

'So where were you?' he demanded.

The secret of my brother's existence was still too personal and too precious to be shared, even with Charlie, so I tried to dodge the question.

'How was the party? How did it go?' I asked as cheerfully as I could.

'Well, there was a great, gaping hole at the table where you were supposed to be sitting,' said Charlie. 'And you didn't even phone or leave a message of apology.'

'Did Sophie have a good time?' I asked.

'She was worried sick,' said Charlie. 'Even I couldn't cheer her up! We seriously considered phoning the police, you know. Or the local hospitals. We thought you'd been in a terrible accident. Apart from that I'm sure she had an absolutely fantastic birthday party, thank you very much!'

'Look, Charlie, I'm really sorry. You know how much I wanted to be there, but something came up. Something very important.'

'What was so important? Tell me, Dave. Help me to understand.'

'I can't tell you about it,' I replied miserably. 'It's something personal.'

'Honestly, Dave, if you can't trust me after all these years, there's no point continuing this conversation. I'm going to bed.'

'Charlie . . . Charlie?' I tried one more time. 'Charlie?' But the line was dead; he had hung up on me.

I redialled the number. I could hear the phone ringing at the other end of the line. 'He's got to answer sooner or later,' I thought.

Eventually he did.

'Charlie, it's Dave,' I said as soon as I heard him pick up.

'Surprise, surprise,' said Charlie bitterly. 'Have you changed your mind? Are you going to tell me why you missed the party?'

'I can't, Charlie – but don't hang up!' I practically shouted. 'You've got to give me Sophie's phone number. I've got to apologise.'

'I don't have her phone number,' said Charlie.

'You must know how to contact her though,' I pleaded.

'I guess I can tell you where she lives,' sighed Charlie. 'Although if I were you I wouldn't turn up there any time soon – her parents were pretty upset.'

In the end he gave me the address and explained how to get there.

'Now leave me alone,' he said, and hung up.

I made my way to bed, struggling with a turmoil of conflicting emotions. I was elated that I'd found Chris and felt full of anticipation about seeing him again, but I was also devastated by Charlie's anger and by the thought that I had hurt Sophie and destroyed any chance of a relationship with her. I decided that as soon as I woke up I must go to her house and make my apologies.

I didn't sleep too late and by mid-morning I was showered and dressed and on my way to apologise to Sophie.

Her house was a small semi and the front garden was surrounded by tall hedges badly in need of a trim. I had often wondered where Sophie lived and frequently imagined visiting her at her house – going to her bedroom to listen to CDs, perhaps progressing on to a quick kiss and then . . . but there was no way that was going to happen in circumstances like these.

I put daydreams out of my mind. Instead I loitered on the far side of the road, debating with myself: 'Should I go through with this? Will my turning up here make things better or worse?'

Before I had made a decision, I heard a car engine start with a cough and a splutter, then the high-pitched whine of a loose belt as the revs increased. There was the crunch of gravel under tyres and Sophie's parents' car emerged, boot first, from their driveway, the leaves and twigs of the hedge scraping down the sides and marking the paint. The car backed out into the road and then pulled up at the kerb outside the house with the engine still running.

I was tempted to hide, but it was too late. Sophie's

father had already seen me. As he started to wind down his window, I walked across the road towards him.

'Oh, so you're still alive then!' said Mr Tanner. 'Good. Would have been nice if you'd let us know the happy news last night though. Would have saved a lot of worry. Not to mention money – I'd already paid for your meal, you know.'

'I'm sorry,' I said. 'I've come to apologise.'

'Well, that's something I suppose.'

Sophie's father sounded more friendly now, but I wasn't looking at him any more. I was looking over his head, down the drive to the front of the house. Sophie had just appeared at the front door. She looked beautiful. Her long hair was hanging down over her shoulders and she wore a simple blue dress that made her look tall and model-like. My heart leapt and suddenly I was glad I had come.

Sophie must have seen me but she didn't move; just stood like a statue in the doorway.

'Do you think I could apologise to Sophie?' I asked.

'I think that would be a very good idea.' Mr Tanner turned off the ignition and climbed out of the car. 'You wait here. I'll go and get her for you.'

I stood nervously fiddling with the buttons on my jacket as he made his way up the drive. He met Sophie in the doorway and they spoke for a few moments. He looked back over his shoulder and nodded at me. Sophie shook her head and turned back into the gloom of the house. My heart sank. Her father made his way back up the drive to see me.

'I'm sorry,' he said. 'We're all about to go out and Sophie's gone to get her coat. She said she doesn't have time to talk to you right now, but she told me to thank you for your apology, and said not to worry about the party.'

I felt as if I had been punched in the stomach. I tried to say something but couldn't get the words out. I hung my head and turned to go.

I must have looked as terrible as I felt because Mr Tanner called out after me.

'Take it from an old-timer like me, Dave – it's not always a bad sign when a woman's angry with you!'

I just carried on walking. What did middle-aged men know about love and rejection?

Later that afternoon I climbed up to a green door and selected the button that would ring the bell upstairs in Chris's flat.

I rang and in an instant the door swung open. To my horror I found an outrageously dressed man on his knees just inside the door. His head was thrown back so far that the veins stood out in his neck, his eyes were screwed tight shut and he had a long-stemmed red rose in his mouth.

'Marry me!' he shouted around the rose stem.

Then he opened his eyes.

'Oh! Slight targeting error. Expecting someone else. Anything I can do?' he asked in a staccato burst of sentences as he clambered to his feet. He towered over me – he must have been at least six foot four – and to my surprise he didn't seem in the least embarrassed.

'I'm l-l-looking for Chris,' I stuttered, and was relieved

to see him appearing out of the gloom in the hallway behind the other man.

'You found us!' said Chris. 'Come on in. You've met Rufus, my wanna-be-famous-musician-but-actually-a-boring-law-student flat mate then?'

'Yeah,' I murmured, totally overawed by my sudden plunge into Chris's social life.

'Hey, introduce us then,' demanded Rufus. 'I did just propose to him, after all. It was an accident,' he added hastily, as Chris spun around, eyebrows raised.

After the introductions, Chris and I climbed the stairs to the flat, while Rufus waited to ambush his girlfriend, Annie. Once inside, Chris boiled a kettle and searched around the messy kitchen for tea bags and milk. Then he went to his bedroom and reappeared with a packet of chocolate biscuits.

'I have to hide anything with chocolate,' he explained. 'Otherwise Rufus eats it.'

The doorbell rang and a few seconds later I heard a second cry of 'Marry me!' and then the mumble of voices and the sound of feet coming up the stairs.

'She turned me down again,' wailed Rufus, as he threw open the kitchen door and pretended to hammer his forehead against the wall. 'The woman has the face of an angel but a heart of stone.'

Over a cup of tea and a packet of chocolate biscuits Rufus and Annie fired question after question at Chris and me, shouting to make themselves heard over the radio station that was blasting out from at least three different stereos dotted around the flat. Every so often Chris or

Rufus would shout for quiet so that a favourite song could be listened to with the attention they felt it deserved, and eventually, after one such interval, there came a time when both the questions and the biscuits had run out and conversation slowed for good.

'We're off to IMPACT at the leisure centre,' announced Rufus standing to his feet and dragging his girlfriend off her chair. 'What are you two up to? You coming?'

'It's up to Dave,' said Chris. 'We still have a lot to catch up on.'

'I'm happy to do whatever you want,' I said, wondering if IMPACT was some kind of violent martial art. If it was, then I was certain I didn't want to be sparring with Chris, and especially not with Rufus.

'Let me explain what you'll be letting yourself in for,' said Chris. 'IMPACT is a Christian event . . .'

'Chris is a bit old for it really,' interjected Rufus helpfully.

'It's held one Sunday evening a month,' continued Chris, ignoring his flat mate. 'There'll be music, dancing and, most likely, some kind of guest speaker. Do you think you'd like to go?'

I opened my mouth but unfortunately my brain hadn't yet decided on its answer and I just stood there, mouth open, like a 16-year-old goldfish.

'I met Annie at IMPACT,' declared Rufus. 'You'd be mad not to give it a go!'

There was no arguing with that kind of logic and I gave in.

'All right, I'll give it a try,' I replied with as much enthusiasm as I could muster. 'It might even be fun.'

I was surprised to find that we had to join a queue that looked at least a mile long before we could gain entry to the event. That messed with my mind for starters. Then there was the problem of the people in the queue. I thought this was supposed to be a Christian event and I had assumed that Christian events would be attended only by old-age pensioners or by cardigan-wearing members of the Young Conservatives Club, yet the people I found myself rubbing shoulders with as we crammed through the doors looked almost normal.

But that was nothing compared to the shock I got after the man on the door stamped my hand and pointed me in the direction of the main sports hall. The music was so loud that it seemed to flow out of the doors of the hall and break over us like a wave. I heard it with my ears but felt it in my chest! Inside, the hall was dark and already packed with people – hundreds of people. I was glad of Rufus's bulk as he shouldered his way through the crowds, clearing a path for us that led in the direction of the main stage. The next hour passed in a flash of loud music, dancing and striking visuals projected onto the walls around the gymnasium.

I had a chance to draw breath when the music stopped and a young woman carried a microphone onto the stage. As the lights came up, I sank gratefully to the floor next to Chris. A young black man climbed up to join the woman on the stage.

'I'd like you to welcome JC,' the young woman announced. 'He's from Chicago. He's a great DJ and a powerful speaker!'

In spite of the loud applause it seemed that JC felt the need to prove his credentials. He walked across the stage to his decks and proceeded to treat us to a virtuoso display of the first of his skills. When the hall finally quietened down and everyone was back on the floor, he started to speak.

Allowing us time to get used to his broad American accent he told us a little about himself and then explained that his subject would be the Holy Spirit.

He first explained to us who the Holy Spirit was: that is, the third person of the Trinity. Along with Jesus and the Father, the Holy Spirit is God. Three in one.

Then we were taken on a whistle-stop tour of the Bible. The Holy Spirit cropped up everywhere, right from the very first chapter of the Old Testament in the account of the creation of the world, through to the New Testament where he became especially active around the time of Jesus. Jesus then promised that the Holy Spirit would be a helper and comforter to his disciples after he himself had died and been taken up to heaven.

'So that's who the Holy Spirit is,' said JC. 'But what does he do? What difference does he make to our lives? What difference does he make to our Christian experience?'

It was surprisingly quiet in the hall and I could see many upturned faces in the brighter light that reflected from the stage – all of them focused on JC and what he had to say.

'The Holy Spirit's work in us is vital. It is by God's Spirit that we are born again as Christians, and it is by God's Spirit that we, the church, are brought together in unity.

It is God's Spirit who gives us the spiritual gifts that are for the good of everyone. It is God's Spirit who helps us to grow both as individuals, becoming more like Jesus, and as a church, calling other people into God's family. But perhaps most importantly it is the Holy Spirit who assures us that we ourselves are part of God's family, that God loves us and that he is our Father.'

I found myself listening to the speaker's voice almost more than his words. Even aside from the accent, it was different – deep and with an uncommon rhythm. If I shut my eyes it reminded me of the American civil rights preachers I had recently seen in a video at school.

'The wonderful news is that by his Holy Spirit we can all know the love of our Father God,' JC continued. 'There is a beautiful and ancient fairy tale that speaks of a king who adopts waifs and strays and makes them princes and princesses. In the same way we are God's adopted sons and daughters, heirs to the King of kings. We too become princes and princesses, members of the first family of the universe.'

The talk was too long for me, and I started looking around at the other people whose faces and forms I could make out around us. Just to Chris's right were three girls of about my age, and one of them, while not as pretty as Sophie, would definitely have attracted Charlie's interest. I looked away quickly when she turned round – it was so embarrassing when a girl caught you looking at her. I tried to refocus my mind.

'The Holy Spirit lives within every person who belongs to Jesus Christ, but not all of us are full of the Spirit. We don't all let him work to the full in our lives. That is like just having the pilot light on in a gas boiler. It shows that the boiler is on, and it shows that the Christian is alive, but it doesn't put out any heat or give any energy. Why should we be happy to have just the pilot light on in our Christian lives when God can cause us to burst into flame?' He left that question hanging in the air for a few seconds and then continued in a quieter voice. 'For those of you who want to know God better, for those of you who need to experience his love, for those of you who simply want more power to live for Christ, in short for any who are willing, there will be an opportunity after the break to be filled again by the Spirit of God.'

He walked to the back of the stage and disappeared out of the spotlights, leaving us, or at least me, to try and decide whether what we had just been offered was a challenge, an invitation or perhaps both.

A few more lights came on throughout the hall and the music started again, though not as loud as previously.

'Great talk,' exclaimed Rufus as we joined the flow of people heading for the refreshment stalls dotted around the outside of the hall.

'What exactly happens if you're filled with the Spirit?' I asked a little later as the four of us stood in a tight circle sipping at our cokes. I was trying hard to conceal the anxiety I felt.

'There's no answer to that,' said Chris. 'Different people are affected in different ways.'

'Because like any good father,' interrupted Rufus, 'God

treats his children as individuals. Whatever happens, it's always just what you need,' he added.

After the break we returned to our seats and JC spoke for a few more minutes and then explained that he was going to lead us in a prayer. He made it very clear that only those who wished to should join in, and there was no pressure or obligation.

I decided that I would give it a go.

'Repeat after me,' said JC. 'Out loud if you want to. If not, just inside – God can still hear you.

'Heavenly Father, I ask that you would forgive me of anything that I have done wrong that might be a barrier to my receiving your Holy Spirit. I want you to know that I'm committed to turning away from anything in my life that displeases you. With all my heart I long to know you and I want the precious gift of your Holy Spirit. Amen.'

I followed along with the speaker in my mind and meant every word. I wanted to be filled with the Holy Spirit. I wanted to experience more of God, but I was also nervous about what would happen.

'I suggest that you all stand up,' said JC. 'It might be an idea to close your eyes and to hold your hands out in front of you, just as you would if you were about to be given a present. There is nothing magical about this position; it is simply body language that helps us to keep our minds focused on what it is we are doing. That is, we are asking to be given something.'

I closed my eyes and raised my hands as he suggested. By now the darkened hall was very quiet. All I could hear was the gentle rasp of people's breathing. I felt peaceful and nervous at the same time and I had a hard time stopping the corners of my mouth twitching up into a smile as JC began to pray again.

'Father, we invite you to send your Holy Spirit to fill us now. We want you and we need you. Please, Holy Spirit, come.'

Once again the hall was quiet and I stood still and silent with the rest. Then gradually something began to happen. I can't describe it to you in detail, it was simply too personal to put into words, but basically I began to feel God; to experience his love and his power in an amazing way. I could sense Chris standing beside me and to my surprise he seemed to be speaking quietly in a foreign language.

Very little time seemed to have passed when I began to hear people moving and the music started up again. While I was still too affected by my experience to talk, a small crowd, including the teenage girls I had watched earlier, began to form around Chris and Rufus. From the way some of the girls were giggling and staring I almost expected them to ask for autographs.

'Is it true that you are going to run the club again?' asked one of the crowd, looking at Chris.

'We hope so,' replied Chris. 'But there are still a lot of details to work out.'

'And will you and your band play again?' one of the girls asked Rufus.

'If we can get the logistics sorted then we might hammer out a couple of numbers,' grinned Rufus. 'But don't worry, we'll let you know what's happening!'

After the meeting, when Chris drove me home to Southerton, I had a number of questions for him.

'Hey Chris, what was that foreign language you were speaking earlier?' I asked the question that most puzzled me.

'A foreign language?' said Chris. 'I don't think so. I have enough problems with English.'

'You were. Definitely.'

'Oh,' said Chris, after a moment's thought. 'I think I know what you heard, but I'm not sure how to explain it to you.' I waited as patiently as I could for Chris to give it a try.

'You heard me praying in tongues,' he began.

'So what's that?' I asked.

'The gift of tongues is one of the gifts that the Holy Spirit gives to Christians,' continued Chris. 'It is as if my spirit inside me is able to communicate exactly what it is feeling to God without the process of passing it through my mind to be translated into English. I know it sounds strange,' said Chris, taking his eyes off the road for long enough to note my quizzical expression, 'but praying in tongues helps to build us up and make us spiritually strong, a bit like using weights can build you up physically. And you can pray in tongues when you really wouldn't know what to pray in English.'

That was about as clear as engine oil as far as I was concerned, but I moved on to my next question anyway.

'And what's the club?'

'The club?' said Chris with a sigh. 'The club is a little project of Rufus and mine that is getting out of control. It started out a year or so ago as a few friends getting together in an old Scout hut to listen to and to play music. Then we made the mistake of inviting young people from local churches to come and join us. Now we have constant demands to run more evenings and a constant struggle to find a venue big enough for everyone who wants to be there.'

'So when's the next one?' I asked. 'Am I invited?'

'Of course you are,' laughed Chris. 'I promise you'll be the first to know about it.' As Chris's car drew to a standstill at the end of my road I asked another question.

'When can I see you again?'

'Any time!' said Chris emphatically. 'Just give me a call or email me.'

Chapter Ten

Monday 12 February, 6.55 pm

That evening I arrived at swimming practice slightly later than usual. Throughout a dreary day at school I had tried to convince myself that everything would work itself out. Sure, Sophie and Charlie were avoiding me and the general atmosphere seemed a little chilly, but I could understand that – I deserved it. In any case a bit of trouble with schoolfriends seemed like a small price to pay for having found a brother. However, as I walked into the changing room I was met by a wall of silence. No one spoke or even looked at me.

'Hi guys,' I said uncertainly.

It was as if I weren't there. No one so much as glanced in my direction and no one said a word. I dumped my bag down beside Charlie.

'Hi,' I said more quietly, just to him.

'Hi,' he replied half-heartedly, then just picked up his goggles and walked out.

In seconds I was the only person left in the changing room. As I struggled out of my uniform and got ready to swim I could hear the usual beginning-of-practice noises coming from the pool. Splashes, shouts, screams and laughs and the echoing babble of excited conversation. I was desperately trying to convince myself that the worrying silence in the changing room hadn't happened, and that as soon as I walked out onto the poolside everything would be normal again. It wasn't.

As I appeared in the doorway the people nearest me stopped talking and the silence spread out across the whole pool area like a ripple. Those in the water swam to the side and climbed out without speaking. Mr Bishop and his assistant coaches, who were holding a huddled conference in one corner, looked up, surprised by the quiet, but then went back to their planning session. I was scared and took a half-step back into the changing room but then decided there was no point in hiding. Instead I stood alone with my back to the wall, waiting for the start of the practice.

As the coach called us together he was obviously confused by the very uncharacteristic silence that surrounded him. 'What's up? Has somebody died?' he asked, trying to take control of a situation he didn't understand.

'We wish!' said Phil, just loud enough for everyone to hear him. There were a few giggles and a stifled laugh, and a number of heads turned to look at me. Unfortunately Mr Bishop also caught sight of me. He needed to shout at someone to prove that he was still in charge and unfortunately I was a convenient target.

'Ah, Dave, nice of you to turn up.'

I had completely forgotten that I had skipped Friday's practice, but now it came back to me, as did the fact that this coach demanded perfect attendance.

'Busy on Friday, were we?' enquired Mr Bishop in a

voice dripping with sarcasm. 'Too much on to bother coming and training with the rest of us? Not even the common decency to let me or one of your friends know you wouldn't be at practice? You'd better shape up or I'll have you off this team in a flash!'

'Dave has a habit of letting people down,' said Phil. 'It might be pathological, some kind of mental disease. What he needs is a lesson in how to treat people. Which is exactly what we're going to give him,' he added more quietly.

'Yes . . . thank you, Phil,' said Mr Bishop, still not sure what was going on. 'We've got a gala coming up soon, and less than seven weeks to the National Schools Championships themselves. Next week is half-term so we'd better get on with the serious business of swimming. Off to your lanes – NOW!' he shouted.

Throughout the practice nobody spoke a word to me. If there was a group of people having a chat between swims the conversation stopped as soon as I approached, and restarted as soon as I left. There was no doubt in my mind that Phil had finally found the ideal opportunity to get at me. For the first time I was vulnerable to him because Charlie was angry with me and did nothing to defend me. Quite what version of events Phil had been telling around school all day I didn't like to think. He had everyone turned against me. What hurt worst of all was Charlie's attitude. He didn't go along with the silent treatment – he replied when I spoke to him and said goodnight when we left – but he wouldn't enter into conversation and went out of his way to avoid having to

walk the same route home. I left alone and thoroughly miserable.

Sunday 25 February, 1.30 pm

As Chris and I drove through some of the scruffier suburbs of the city in his beaten-up old car I thought back over the past two weeks since I had first met him. They had been the best and worst of times.

The absolute low point had been last Wednesday, Valentine's Day. Perhaps the worst day in my entire school career to date. Of course Valentine's has never been my favourite day as I have always suffered from a marked lack of cards falling onto my doormat, but that Valentine's was far worse. For a start the wall of silence that Phil had erected around me at the swimming club seemed to affect the whole school – it seemed that I was not to be spoken to under any circumstances. The highlight of my day was when a fellow student forgot the rule and asked me how to answer a homework question he had neglected to do.

But the silence wasn't the worst of it. Sophie spent the day carting a huge bouquet of at least a dozen red roses around with her from class to class. They had appeared on her desk that morning. To her credit she seemed embarrassed by them and eventually dumped them for the school secretary to look after. Of course they were sent anonymously, but all the smart money was on Phil Squire. Who else could afford dozens of red roses on Valentine's Day?

Throughout the rest of the week Phil had continued to make my life as miserable as possible. He never missed an opportunity to make a joke at my expense or to criticise me – for something as small as my pronunciation of a French verb, or as personal as my appearance. Inevitably his comments affected the way people thought about me and I found myself slipping into the black hole of loneliness that just recently I thought I had avoided for good. Charlie kept well away from me, and we had not talked on any kind of personal level since the night of the party. Even worse, with me out of the picture Sophie, Sunita, Charlie and Phil seemed to be a constant foursome. I tried not to think what they might have been getting up to throughout the long week of half-term.

On the other hand, Chris and I were getting on fantastically well, and that kept me sane in spite of everything. For 13 years neither of us had had a brother or any very close family, and now we were making up for it. He also introduced me to his huge circle of friends, and as they welcomed me into their world I found the strength to carry on in spite of the loneliness I felt at home and school.

That afternoon Chris and I were driving to join some of his friends on a project they were taking part in. Young Christians had been asked by a local charity to join together to clean up a housing estate in a depressed area of the city. I was happy to get involved.

Chris and I drew into the car park that was the designated meeting spot. Already the place was filling up. Teenagers and young adults were pouring in and climbing out of coaches, minibuses and private cars. I spotted

Rufus – never one to blend into a crowd – and when I waved he came over to join us.

In time the workers were assembled and the project leader began to explain the various jobs we would be undertaking. I didn't imagine that I would be leading any of the work groups and so I switched off from the sound of his voice and took the opportunity to scan the people I was going to be working with.

Every stream of youth culture seemed to be represented. Judging by the clothes, the hairstyles and the music that boomed out from half-a-dozen portable or car stereos, I managed to positively identify skateboarders, indie music lovers, clubbers, academics and football fanatics, as well as a host of others who, like me, could not be placed into any of the more obvious categories.

I saw the group of girls that I had first seen at the IMPACT event. They kept glancing in our direction, but I could tell it wasn't me they were looking at. At first I thought it was Chris – I hate the way teenage girls always go for older men – then I realised it was actually Rufus they were making eyes at. I guess he could be considered kind of good-looking, assuming the tight 'Barbie in Hollywood' T-shirt and the baggy pink shorts didn't put you off.

'Aren't you cold?' I asked him.

'I am now, but I won't be as soon as we start work,' he said. I guess he was just one of those people who play life by their own rules.

'We'd best go join our team,' said Chris, setting off down an alleyway in pursuit of our group.

The afternoon was busy. Our team was charged with painting over the graffiti that covered the walls of the community centre in the middle of the estate. Rufus was right, it was hard work, and when the sunshine slanted down to us between the tower blocks I began to sweat. What with all the chat between the different workers, it was some time before I had any opportunity to ask Chris the questions that had been plaguing me. As we sat on a bench, taking a brief break from our painting, I tried to put my thoughts into words.

'Chris, I'm confused,' I began. 'I'm starting to feel as if I'm living in two different worlds. One, the Christian one, is great. There are good people like you and Rufus and I have a lot of fun. Best of all, I feel like I am getting to know God – the Bible is making more sense to me, and when I pray I can really believe that he hears me. But at school things seem to be getting worse and worse, and the love and happiness I've seen in people's lives here just makes the coldness at home more unbearable.' I didn't want to sound as if I were moaning, so I tried to put my question more clearly. 'I don't understand how the world, or even my own life, can be so good and so bad all at once.'

'The world is a strange place,' said Chris. 'And it's certainly not perfect – not even for Christians. I'm sorry about the trouble you're having at school, but I'm afraid that there is no easy way through it. You can't snap your fingers and expect everything to be wonderful just because you are a Christian.'

'So why didn't God make the world perfect?'

'Ever heard of Satan?' asked Chris.

'You're kidding,' I couldn't stop myself from laughing. 'Surely you don't believe all that Stephen King horror movie stuff?'

'Forget the forked tail, the horns and the three-pointed spear,' replied Chris. 'What you're left with is real. Satan is a spiritual being whose aim is to hurt and destroy the thing that God loves most – us.'

Chris was getting ahead of me. I was still having difficulty wrapping my head around the idea that the devil was anything more than an old wives' tale. I tried again.

'You can't tell me that all Christians believe in the devil.'

'Most do,' said Chris. 'The Bible is pretty clear about Satan and the fallen angels that follow him, and it commands us to avoid anything that might bring us into contact with them.'

The conversation was getting more and more bizarre. Two minutes ago we had been talking about trouble at school and now we were onto fallen angels! I was intrigued though, and by now I knew for sure that Chris was no nutcase, so I asked another question.

'Surely people can't contact demons, or fallen angels, or whatever you call them,' I said.

'They can,' replied Chris, 'but they might not know that's what they're doing. You hear all the time about ouija boards, tarot cards, hypnotism, seances, horoscopes – I bet there are people at your school who are into them – but all of those things can bring contact with occult forces. I could go on all day telling you stories about people whose lives have been messed up by playing about like that.'

I was still a bit sceptical, but also glad that those things had never featured in my list of crazes. For a moment or two there was silence as we stood up from the bench, collected our brushes and returned to the section of wall we were painting. It seemed to me that the elements themselves were listening in on our conversation. The sun had moved behind a cloud and the estate, bright with light just moments before, now seemed dark and sinister. I shivered as I dipped my brush and took my place beside Chris.

'Don't get me wrong. I'm not saying you can blame all your problems at school on the devil – that would be stupid. But the devil does attack Christians, particularly new Christians. He'll want to fill your mind with doubts: about God and Christianity and about yourself. You told me about times when you feel really bad about yourself – that you're worthless or stupid. That could well be the devil. He'll also try to tempt you to disobey God and damage your relationship with him. He might tempt you to hate Phil, to blame him for all your troubles, or he might tempt you to feel bitter against Charlie for the way he's treated you. Those are the kinds of things the devil uses to try to get at you.'

'Well, that's just great!' I said sarcastically. 'I feel really happy now.'

'Don't worry,' laughed Chris. 'When it comes to Satan against God we're talking non-league minnows taking on Manchester United. Satan is always going to get flattened. In fact he already has been flattened. The cross was the climax of Satan's big plan to destroy God, but when

Jesus rose from the dead he humiliated Satan in the worst possible way. There are now two kingdoms in the world, and as Christians, the children of God, we have moved from the kingdom of darkness where the devil rules into God's kingdom of love and light. To go back to football, it's as though we've been transferred. We no longer play for the devil, he's not our manager any more, so we have nothing to fear from him.'

I considered that for a minute or two.

'That makes me feel a bit better,' I admitted to Chris.

As we took it in turns to apply the last few splashes of paint to our section of the wall, a shaft of sunlight struck down past the tower blocks to reach us where we stood.

Friday 2 March, 9.30 pm

I sat rolling my desk chair back and forth and fiddling with the phone unit I held cradled in my lap.

The school week that followed half-term had passed slowly. I was still the number one social outcast and while I tried not to admit it, even to myself, the fact was that I was painfully lonely. Eventually Friday had arrived.

Around lunchtime, as I walked alone down the hallway, I had been startled by a tap on my shoulder. I spun around, half-expecting a cruel practical joke. It was Charlie. He didn't say anything but strode into an empty classroom that opened off the hallway. I followed him in.

Charlie launched into what was obviously a pre-prepared speech. 'Phil is an idiot and a creep,' he said. 'Hanging around with him is starting to make me physically sick. I only do it because someone has to keep Sophie and Sunita out of his evil clutches,' he added, by way of an explanation. 'Look, Dave, I want you to be my friend again, but first you're going to have to come clean. I need to know what's going on. I need to know why you didn't come to the party, and why you feel you can't trust me. Think about it and if you're willing to be honest, meet me in the park at two tomorrow afternoon. If you don't come I'll just have to put up with Phil.'

He had walked back out into the hallway and off to his next class before I had a chance to say a word in response to his outburst. I stood in silent thought for a minute. I knew immediately that I would have to talk to Chris and that was why I had returned home after swimming practice and was now seated in my bedroom with my phone on my lap trying to work out how best to convince Chris that Charlie should know the truth.

Up until that point I had kept my brother's existence from everyone. It was a closely guarded secret. But I knew that in order to give Charlie the explanation he needed I would have to tell him everything.

'Do you trust him?' Chris asked me when I explained the situation to him over the phone.

'Absolutely,' I replied. 'He has never let me down in all the years I've known him. I owe him so much. I think I ought to be honest with him.'

But I could tell that Chris was worried by the idea. His next question made clear to me what bothered him.

'What if he lets something slip to your mum or dad?' he asked.

I realised that he was still torn between a desire to see them and his fear that they might reject him yet again or even forbid us from seeing one another. I tried to reassure him by promising that I would explain to Charlie how important secrecy was. In the end Chris agreed quite readily. I think he was curious about meeting Charlie for himself.

As soon as I put the phone down, I began to plan exactly what I would tell Charlie when we met in the park the next day.

Chapter Eleven

Saturday 3 March, 2.00 pm

As I walked towards the park to meet Charlie, the sun was shining from a blue sky dotted with fast-travelling white clouds. The weather inspired optimism and I was confident that Charlie and I could sort out our differences. Not being able to talk to him over the last few weeks had been more painful than all the other insults and silences put together – more painful even than having to return to watching Sophie from a distance. Now I was eager to put the past behind us.

I was still worried enough to fling up a short prayer to God as I walked through the park gates. 'Please God,' I prayed, 'give me the words to say. Help Charlie to understand that I didn't mean to hurt him or Sophie. Please let us be friends again. Amen.'

I caught sight of Charlie sitting alone on a bench in the middle of the park. He was wringing his hands as he watched two squirrels scrabbling in the dirt. That wasn't like Charlie. He almost looked nervous. As I dropped down onto the bench beside him he sat still and silent. For obvious reasons I was rather sensitive to being ignored and for a few painful seconds I worried that he might have changed his mind. Then, without warning and without turning to look at me, he started speaking.

'Dave, I am so sorry,' he began. It was obvious from his tone how serious he was. 'I've been doing a lot of thinking in the last few days and I realise I've treated you badly. I'll understand if you say you don't want to be my friend any more.'

'What?' I was shocked. I had expected to be the one doing all the apologising.

'Hear me out,' continued Charlie. 'However wrong of you it was to not turn up at the party, the way I've treated you for the past three weeks has been unforgivable. Will you let me explain myself?'

'Of course,' I replied. 'Only there is nothing to explain. I deserved everything I got.'

'No you didn't,' said Charlie. 'It's just that I feel so protective of Sophie. There is something different about her. She seems too gentle, too kind for our school and our friends. I hate to see her hurt. I care about her in spite of the fact that she is the only girl I can't make fall for me, no matter how hard I try,' he added with a grin and a glimmer of his usual humour. 'And I know you probably think I have loads of friends; I do I suppose, but no one else like you. I was angry when you wouldn't tell me what was going on, and I felt that for the first time I had been cut out of a part of your life.'

'How does Sophie feel about me now?' I blurted out. I know it was probably unfair on Charlie, but I simply couldn't stop myself. I needed to know. Sophie still haunted my dreams. I couldn't get her out of my mind and I couldn't bear to have hurt her.

'Oh, she's still angry with you. But she feels as bad as I do about the way you've been treated. I promise you it was all Phil's doing and none of ours.'

'I believe you,' I said. 'Now let me explain my side of the story. Perhaps it will help you to understand why I behaved the way I did.'

As I told Charlie all that had happened since I found the secret file in my parents' safe his jaw dropped until it was practically resting on his chest.

'So you see what incredibly bad timing it was that made me miss the party,' I concluded. 'You do understand, don't you, that I couldn't have turned down the chance to meet my brother?'

'You've got a brother!' was all Charlie could manage to say.

When we were younger Charlie and I had often pretended to be brothers. For two only children like us the relationship between real blood brothers had seemed like a mystical bond – so much better than mere friendship.

'I can't believe you've gone and found yourself a brother,' he repeated. 'That's as good as winning the lottery! So when can I meet him?' he asked after barely a moment's pause.

'Soon, I hope,' I said. 'But it's not as simple as all that. There are complications.'

I told Charlie more of Chris's story and explained the need for total secrecy.

'I have to hand it to you,' said Charlie. 'I hoped that you

would have a decent excuse, but I never dreamed any-thing like this was going on. It's incredible. But there's something I still don't understand. I know we haven't spoken for the last two weeks, but I've watched you – closely. You're different. More so than can be explained by your finding a long lost brother. It's inside you.'

It's funny, but sometimes other people can see you better than you can see yourself. As Charlie spoke I knew that what he said was true. I *had* changed, and I knew what had changed me. I had been wrong when I had thought that it was just my newfound brother who had helped me through the last weeks. It was God. It had to be. But could I tell Charlie about that? I thought not.

Later that evening I was sitting with Chris in his car. We were parked down a side street about a ten-minute walk from my home. It was his practice to drop me off before we got too close to the house and to the danger of a dis-astrous chance meeting with my parents.

'Should I have told him about God and Christianity?' I asked.

'When it comes to talking about Christianity,' said Chris, 'there are two common mistakes. Some people go the religious maniac route – they're so keen to tell the good news that they make everyone around them feel uncomfortable. Talking to a religious maniac is almost like going to the dentist – they're up to their elbows in your mouth trying to shove their beliefs down your throat. At the other extreme, people become "secret Christians". They creep through life, silently embarrassed by the deep, dark secret of their faith. From what you've told me I think you're more likely to suffer from the second condition.'

'I'm not really afraid of telling Charlie,' I defended myself. 'It's just that I didn't know what to say, or even whether it was a good idea to say anything.'

As I spoke a car drove past and Chris seemed to sink down into his seat. Being anywhere near my parents' house always made him nervous.

'Of course you should talk about it,' said Chris, sitting up straighter. 'Jesus commanded his followers to tell others. I bet you'd tell Charlie if you won the lottery or something, so why hide this?'

I laughed. It seemed that both Chris and Charlie were obsessed with the lottery.

'What's so funny?' asked Chris.

I explained.

'It looks to me as if you've been given an opening big enough to drive a bus through,' said Chris. 'If Charlie's already noticed the difference in you and is asking questions, all you have to do is be honest.'

'But what about theology?' I asked. 'What if Charlie's got lots of questions? I've only been a Christian a few weeks – I don't know a thing.'

'I don't think you need to worry about that,' said Chris. 'From what you've told me about Charlie I think he lives by his instincts and his feelings. I think you know as well as I do that he's unlikely to start quoting Plato or Socrates at you.'

'He probably thinks Plato's a cartoon character,' I admitted.

'Well then,' said Chris. 'I guess you've got no excuse.'

'Perhaps I should take him to church or something?'

'Would he go?' asked Chris.

'Normally, no way,' I said. 'His mum used to drag him to church and he hated it. But I think that he would do anything for the chance to meet you. If we set it up so that he could meet you at a time when we just happened to be going to church, I'm sure he'd come.'

'I wouldn't want to trick him into coming,' said Chris. 'But we'll think about it. It's not a bad idea to take him to hear someone who is an expert at presenting Christianity.'

'An expert sounds like a good idea to me.'

'Maybe, but you still have to do your bit. Talk to him if you get a chance. If not, you can pray, and that's as important as anything. Ask God to open Charlie's eyes to see that he is real and working in the world today. Pray that God will give you the right words to say when you try to talk to him about what has happened to you.'

As I walked home after saying goodbye to Chris, I was filled with an incredible sense of joy. I could tell that God was with me and I couldn't get over how much I had changed in the last few weeks. I had so much more hope now, so much more peace, and so much more confidence in myself.

As I strolled home through the quiet and the darkness I was in no hurry to reach the house. I whispered two words of prayer over and over again: 'Thank you. Thank you. Thank you.'

Friday 9 March, 4.15 pm

On Friday night the coach pulled out of the school gates carrying the swimming team to our second gala of the term. I had told Charlie that I wanted to speak to him privately, away from all of our other friends, and for that reason we were seated unusually close to the front of the coach, surrounded by the most junior swimmers.

I had prayed a lot about this conversation and I desperately hoped it would go well. I knew that underneath all his confidence and vitality Charlie had a need for God just like mine. He had never known his father and, however doting his mother was, I knew he lacked a purpose and a goal for his life. Perhaps that was why he lived so much from day to day and from girl to girl. I guess that every human being has a need for God but many never realise what it is, or rather who it is, that is missing from their lives. I knew that I would not deserve to be called Charlie's friend if I didn't try to describe to him all that had happened to me.

'So what's the big secret this time?' said Charlie. 'Don't tell me you've gone and found yourself a sister to complete the family set.'

'No, it's nothing like that,' I replied. 'It's got to do with what you said the other day. About the change in me.'

'So I was right,' said Charlie. 'Something else has happened to you. Is it a girl?' he asked. 'That would be great.'

'No, it's not, Charlie! It's more serious than that and better than that.'

'Better than a girl?' said Charlie. 'You've got me there.'

'Please don't joke,' I said. 'This is hard for me to talk about, and I have a feeling that you'll think I've gone mad.'

'Hey, sorry,' said Charlie. 'Go ahead. I'm listening.' He folded his hands in his lap and tilted his head to one side. I couldn't tell if he was making fun of my seriousness or really trying to listen.

I thought back to my talks with Chris over the last few days. We had decided that the best thing was for me to tell Charlie my story. I needed to fit in the way I had been before I met with God, the way I had met him, and the difference he had made to me. I launched into my account, starting with the arrival of the computer disk.

'Let me get this straight,' said Charlie as I finished speaking. 'You're telling me that you've gone religious; become a Christian?'

'More or less,' I agreed.

'Wow,' said Charlie. 'I never would have guessed. If you'd told me you were about to run off with one of the female teachers I couldn't have been more surprised. I suppose this means that you're going to become a priest and that this is the end of all our fun together?'

'Charlie, be serious. I haven't even been to church yet. It's just that, however unbelievable it seems, I've somehow met God, and he's changed me. Incredibly, if I was given the choice, I'd rather live with the silent treatment at school for the next ten years than go back to my life as it was before I became a Christian.'

'There's never a dull moment with you these days,' said Charlie at last. 'I'm pleased for you, but I hope you're not thinking I might be wanting to join the "God squad" too. Religion is not for me. I think it might cramp my style.'

That was obviously the end of the conversation, and Charlie very deliberately changed the subject. Sensing that this would not be a good time to press too hard I gave in and took to quizzing him about the teams we would be swimming against. This group of schools would provide tougher competition than at the last gala, but Charlie assured me we still had a good chance of winning.

I was relieved that in spite of Mr Bishop's threat to throw me off the team I had kept my place. There had even been a rumour going around that if the coach hadn't been angry with me for missing a practice he might have selected me for the individual breaststroke events instead of Phil. I was quite happy still to be on the medley relay team. That was quite enough pressure for me.

It seemed like *déjà-vu*. Once again I was sitting next to Charlie on a bench at the poolside while my stomach tied itself into tight little knots.

'OK. Team talk,' called Mr Bishop during a break between races. We all gathered around him. 'Well done to everybody who has swum so far,' he began. 'You should all be proud of your performances. With just the senior relays to go, you've put us in an excellent position. Some of you will already know that the results of this gala are very important. They will decide our ranking for the National Schools Gala at the end of this month. The better we do here, the better we'll be ranked, and the better we're ranked the easier path we'll be given through the early heats.'

'I think I'm going to be sick,' I whispered into Charlie's ear.

'So just go out there and do your best. We'll be cheering for you,' finished the coach.

The swimmers for our race were called and soon I found myself standing with Charlie in our now familiar position at the end of the pool.

'Just like last time,' said Charlie. 'Swim like that again and we've got this race and this gala sewn up.'

'I hope,' I replied, as I stepped forward to grip the edge of the pool with my toes.

The gun went off and Justin started to plough a furrow up the pool straight towards me. As I concentrated harder, the yells and the cheering faded from my hearing and I focused on the lane ahead of me. Justin touched, I dived, and my body sliced through the water like a knife. One stroke under the water and then back to the surface and onwards. I could tell that I was swimming well; better than that, I was swimming like a dream. I felt strong and relaxed and fast. I watched out of the corner of my eye and saw that each stroke was pulling me further ahead of the other swimmers. As I approached the end, I stole a longer look to my right to see where the second-placed swimmer was. Still watching to my right I stretched forward with my left hand and touched the cold hard concrete of the pool's end. Phil's body flew over me, momentarily shading me from the bright lights above, and I stood to my feet in excitement. We should win this one.

As I reached up to pull myself from the water I looked up into the eyes of the lane judge. In a split second all my elation died and was replaced by despair. I climbed out of the pool and unwanted tears of anger and frustration sprang up to sting my eyes as I watched the lane judge raise her flag above her head. The little red flag proclaimed a simple but devastating message: 'Southerton Comprehensive disqualified for an illegal touch on the breaststroke leg.'

It was the oldest mistake in the book and I couldn't believe that I had been stupid enough to make it. Breaststroke swimmers must touch with both hands simultaneously, but I had touched only with my left. The lane judge had seen it and disqualified not just me, but the whole relay team.

Charlie finished in first place and joyfully pulled himself out of the pool thinking we'd won.

Slowly, people began to notice the flag. The second-placed team were the first to comprehend and they wasted no time in starting to celebrate their good fortune. For a second or two Charlie watched them with a puzzled look on his face, then I had to watch his expression change as the painful truth hit him. Soon an official announcement was made and the whole arena knew that we had been disqualified.

We took no points from that relay and slipped right

down the table. In the end we finished the gala ranked a disappointing fourth out of eight school teams.

I sat in silence in the changing room. Charlie was beside me, bravely trying to hide his disappointment.

'It could have happened to anyone, Dave. In fact it has happened to most of us. Don't take it personally. No one blames you,' he said.

But they did blame me, and even worse I blamed myself. I sat stewing in my anger and frustration.

Inevitably Phil chose that moment to make an appearance and a point. He stood before me with his hands on his hips and water still dripping from his hair.

'What were you thinking?'

I stayed silent and Phil swore at me.

'Leave him alone, Phil,' said Charlie standing to his feet. 'Don't you think he feels bad enough already?'

'No, I don't,' said Phil warming to his task as other people crowded around us. 'I just want to make certain that Davey realises he's destroyed our chance at Nationals – wasted a year's work.'

As Phil spoke, something snapped in me. The anger and frustration that had been directed inwards suddenly found a more satisfying target. In a silent rage I stood to my feet. Wordlessly I grabbed Phil by the waist and arm and threw him spinning away from me.

It wasn't a particularly dangerous move and everything would have been OK if the floor of the changing room hadn't been so wet. Shocked and surprised by my violent response, Phil was thrown helplessly off balance. He tried desperately to recover, but his attempt to halt his dizzy progress across the changing room caused his foot to slip and he fell awkwardly onto one knee. The kneecap struck the tiled floor with a loud crack.

His cry of pain changed the atmosphere in the room. Charlie pushed his way through the other swimmers to Phil's side.

'Phil, are you OK?' he asked.

As I looked through the press of bodies, I saw Phil lying on the ground clutching his knee. His face was twisted in pain.

Chapter Twelve

Sunday 11 March, 2.05 pm

'I'm sick of Philip Squire,' I told Chris. 'The world would be a better place without him in it. Why does he have to pick on me all the time? Why can't he leave me alone?'

Chris was sitting opposite me in a small restaurant that offered an 'all you can eat buffet' for Sunday lunch. After four or five servings Chris had finally finished his meal. He was fiddling with the salt and pepper pots in the middle of the table as I moaned on and on about Philip and about the trouble I was sure to be in, at school and at home, as a result of what had happened at the gala.

When my whining finally stopped he didn't respond for a while. Then, when he spoke, he spoke slowly and quietly.

'Dave,' he said, 'we've had some good times together over the past few weeks. So I'm going to tell you what I really think. Consider my honesty a sign of respect – of friendship.'

I didn't particularly like the tone. It was sympathy I was looking for.

Chris continued: 'From what you've told me about your trouble with Phil, I can't help feeling that you must take some of the blame.'

'What?' I cried. 'You must be joking! Phil has treated me like dirt all of this term.'

Chris just raised his hands, palms towards me, and waited for me to quieten down. Then he continued.

'If I remember rightly, you first had a problem when you kicked his pen across the examination room floor,' said Chris.

I cursed myself for having told him that story, and looking back I seemed to remember that I'd even laughed a bit, gloating about my getting away with it while he got into trouble. Sure enough, Chris had remembered that as well.

'No wonder he was upset – he was the one who ended up in detention.'

I started to defend myself. 'Look, I tried . . .'

'Hold on,' said Chris, overruling my protests. 'Let me finish. I agree he reacted badly. There's no excusing that. But look at this latest situation. You're angry and are blaming him, but you're the one who got violent and he's the one who ended up in hospital getting his bruised kneecap X-rayed.'

I sat in silence with my head down, staring at the empty plates on the table in front of me. It didn't sound too good when it was put like that.

'You might be right,' I said finally, in a strangled voice. 'Sorry, Chris. I'm not much of a Christian, am I?'

'Being a Christian is not about being perfect,' said Chris, 'or we'd all be in trouble. But we should face up to our failings and, especially where they affect other people, put them right.'

I guessed where this was heading.

'Don't ask me to apologise,' I pleaded. 'Everyone would think I'd done it because I was scared of him. I might as well kiss his shiny black shoes. I'd be the school joke!'

'I can't make you do anything,' said Chris, shrugging and looking around for the waiter.

In desperation I tried to think up objections, but couldn't conjure up anything that wouldn't sound like a lame excuse.

Monday 12 March, 4.15 pm

The geography classroom was warm and quiet. I was sitting alone on the back row, looking at the maps that lined the walls and wondering if there was anywhere in the whole world as boring as that classroom. In front of me was a scattering of the school's less desirable elements. Hoping to pass the time, I tried to guess what they were in detention for.

Trevor was from my year and a known dopehead. Perhaps a teacher had finally realised what the little tin in his back pocket contained. I didn't know any of the others, but the girl on the front row had a torn shirt and a bruise on her mouth. It didn't take Sherlock Holmes to guess why she was here. Mr Bishop had told me that after injuring Phil so badly I was lucky to have got away with nothing more than a week of detentions, but a week seemed like an eternity just then.

I was bored, and after checking that the teacher wasn't looking I carefully reached into my bag and pulled out the small New Testament that Chris had given me. It was written in a much more modern form of English than the old Bible I had on my bookshelves; better still, it looked like a normal paperback so there was little danger of my being discovered. I flicked through to the beginning of Luke's Gospel – the point I had reached in my Bible reading.

Possibly it was a guilty reaction to injuring Phil's leg, but as I read through chapters 4 and 5 one thing struck me again and again. Jesus seemed to spend an amazing amount of his time healing people. There was the mother-in-law of his disciple Peter, the man with the skin disease, the paralytic who was lowered through a hole in the roof like some sort of disabled Ethan Hawke from *Mission Impossible*.

In the past I had always assumed that the miracles in the Bible were made-up stories, but now, after my own experiences of God, I wasn't so sure. As the detention period came to an end I decided to ask Chris what he thought about healing and miracles.

'Of course I believe in healing,' replied Chris when I raised the subject on the phone that night.

'But you've never actually seen a healing, right?'

'Sure I have,' said Chris. 'But nothing so dramatic as the things Jesus did, I admit.'

'So you can't prove that the things you saw were miracles.'

'No,' said Chris, 'I can't prove it, but I have no doubt that it was God who was healing people.'

'This is weird.'

'Why so surprised? You're the one telling me the Bible's full of miracles and healing.'

'But maybe that's different,' I was thinking out loud. 'Jesus was God, after all, and we're just normal people.'

'We're certainly not Jesus,' agreed Chris. 'But he promised he'd give us the power to do the same things he did.'

There was a pause – one of those sudden lulls you get when chatting on the phone. In the silence I could vaguely make out the distant echo of another conversation somehow bleeding into our phone line. I was distracted, straining to hear what the strangers were talking about.

Chris must have interpreted my silence as doubt or disagreement.

'Don't worry, I'm not trying to sell you some "faith healer" nonsense. There have been miraculous healings all through the history of the church. In fact in the Old Testament God even named himself "the one who heals".'

Chris paused as though waiting for me to ask another question or make another comment. I stayed silent.

'I tell you what,' he said after a moment. 'What you need is some first-hand experience. There's an old lady in our church who is very ill, and I'm supposed to be going to see her tomorrow evening. You don't swim on Tuesdays, so why don't you come with me?'

Tuesday 13 March, 8.00 pm

Even with the lights on, Mrs Gladstone's house was dim and musty, a bit like a cave, and full of old-fashioned pictures and furniture. The lady who had let us in was dressed in a blue and white uniform.

'You know the way,' she said to Chris. 'I'll be having a quick cup of tea in the kitchen. Call me if you need anything.'

Mrs Gladstone was lying in bed with her eyes shut when Chris and I tiptoed into her room. Chris glanced at me, putting a finger to his lips to indicate that I should be quiet. We were not quiet enough. The old lady woke up.

'Come in, my dears. I'm not asleep, and I've been looking forward to your visit all day. Why don't you come and sit yourselves here?' She slid a thin arm out from under the covers and motioned to two seats beside her bed.

Having been introduced, I slipped into a world of my own thoughts, leaving Chris and Mrs Gladstone to chat together about their church and the many friends they had in common. I looked around her bedroom. Every surface was cluttered with the trinkets, pictures and mementos that Mrs Gladstone had accumulated through her long lifetime. There was also a great deal of medicine in the room. Numerous bottles of pills stood on her bedside table, and in one corner stood a large oxygen canister with tubes and a mask attached. It was obvious that this was a seriously ill woman. Chris had told me that she had a bad heart and I began to worry that our prayers would be useless.

Chris and Mrs Gladstone tried to draw me into their conversation, but I was too nervous to take much part. I was relieved when half an hour later Chris brought the chat to an end.

'I'm afraid we can't stay much longer, Mrs Gladstone,' he said. 'I have to drive Dave back to Southerton. But we'd love to pray for you before we go. Would that be OK?'

'Of course, my dear,' she said. 'I'd be terribly disappointed if you didn't.'

My hands began to sweat a little. I couldn't bear the thought that nothing would happen; that her high expectations would be dashed. I also worried that when nothing happened they would blame me. I wasn't a good enough or an old enough Christian to be praying for people with heart conditions.

'This is all new to Dave,' Chris told Mrs Gladstone. 'Is it OK if I explain things to him as we go along?'

Mrs Gladstone nodded.

'Great,' said Chris, encouraging me with a smile. 'Is there anything in particular that we can pray for you, Mrs Gladstone? Apart from your heart, I mean.'

'Well dear, I have been feeling exceptionally tired lately,' she said. 'Everything seems such an effort. I'd appreciate it if you could ask the good Lord to give me more strength.'

'Of course,' said Chris. Then he turned to me. 'Now that we know what Mrs Gladstone wants prayer for we can begin. Remember there's no magic formula: God heals, we just do the asking. What's important is that we pray in a way that Mrs Gladstone finds comfortable. In the Bible people often placed a hand on the person they were praying for.'

He took Mrs Gladstone's hand as he said this, and immediately began to pray.

To my surprise his prayer was soft and quiet. I had been expecting something more dramatic. Unlike me, Chris didn't seem to feel any pressure. He simply prayed that God would send his Holy Spirit to come and touch Mrs Gladstone, and he asked that he would heal her heart and give her more strength to live life. He finished his prayer by saying that all that he asked he asked in the name of Jesus.

I couldn't believe it was all over. It had been so simple, so gentle. 'That's not going to do any good,' I thought.

I noticed that Mrs Gladstone was looking at me.

'You're worried that Chris's prayer won't be answered?' she asked. I nodded, surprised at how easily she had been able to read my thoughts. 'You don't have to worry; I know without a shadow of a doubt that one day I'll be healed. The only question is whether God heals me before or after I die!' She laughed – actually it was more of a wheezy chuckle – as she said this and I was surprised to note that she seemed totally unafraid of death. 'We all have to die some time, dear,' she continued. 'I've lived a full life and I've been a Christian for many, many years, so it's not such a terrible prospect. I know I'll be well again in my new home in heaven. In the meantime just having wonderful young people like yourself and your brother come to visit me is a sign of God's love and care for me.

You really mustn't feel sorry for me, Dave. I know I am safe in the good Lord's hands.'

Long after we had left her house, even after Chris had dropped me back in Southerton, the image of Mrs Gladstone's peaceful face and the memory of her words stayed in my mind. They showed me, more clearly than anything Chris could have said, what a wonderful security came from knowing God and being a Christian.

Reflecting on all that God had done for me over the past few weeks, I decided that the least I could do for him would be to give Philip Squire the apology he undoubtedly deserved. I was grateful to Chris for not having mentioned it again, but even without his prompting I knew what was right.

Wednesday 14 March, 12.55 pm

Almost to my surprise, I found myself standing on the shadowed side of a small, quiet courtyard in the school grounds. I stood with my back to the wall in a position that was at least partly hidden from any observer's view by a cluster of six-foot-tall dustbins. They stood ready to be collected by the local council. Under my breath I was muttering to myself, 'I must be crazy. I can't believe I'm even considering this . . .'

I was watching Phil, who was sitting alone on a bench on the far side of the courtyard as far away as possible from the poisonous-smelling dustbins. He was facing me but had his eyes shut and his head back as he relaxed in the rays of early spring sunshine. His crutches were propped up on the bench beside him and his injured leg was stretched out frontwards, resting on the top of his expensive leather briefcase.

Even alone and obviously injured he seemed to represent everything I was not. Effortlessly successful, used to being in control, perfectly groomed and dressed, popular and influential . . . and spending loads of time with Sophie!

I grimaced. Hard as I tried to forget about Sophie, she still invaded my thoughts frequently and unexpectedly. I continued to watch her as we sat in classes, studying her face and hoping desperately for the forgiving smile that never materialised. Instead I had to endure the torture of seeing her laughing and talking with Phil.

Phil – there were a million reasons why I hated him, but I knew I owed him an apology. More time passed and still I stood quiet and hidden. Secretly I think I hoped that someone would come and join Phil, making it impossible for us to talk alone. In the end my hand was forced by the arrival of our less-than-friendly school caretaker.

'Oi! What are you doing hanging around my dustbins? Probably smoking, aren't you? Full of young delinquents this school is,' he raved. 'Now just clear off before I get a teacher to sort you out.'

He wagged his finger threateningly at me before moving off to do whatever it is that school caretakers do.

Phil, alerted to the fact that he was not alone by the caretaker's carrying-on, raised a hand to shield his eyes from the sun and so get a better view of the situation. When he saw me an ugly expression appeared on his face.

'Not a great start,' I thought.

'Just get lost, Johnson,' called Phil. 'I want nothing to do with you.'

I kept walking towards him, fighting back my desire to give up on this as a bad job.

'I've come to apologise,' I said.

'Finally!' said Phil. 'I'd have gone to the police and had you charged with assault if I'd known the school would let you off with a couple of detentions. You put me on crutches!'

I tried not to respond to his taunts but I was both angry and scared. In my mind I tried to pray but couldn't collect my thoughts enough. I ploughed on.

'Look, I'm sorry. I lost my temper and I shouldn't have. You have to understand I never really meant to hurt you.'

'What do you think this is – infants' school?' asked Phil scornfully. 'I'm not going to shake hands and forget all about it. An apology doesn't alter the fact that I can barely walk and might not be back to swimming in time for the Nationals. You've said your piece, now get lost. I'm sick of the sight of you.'

I made one last attempt. 'Phil, I'm sorry,' I repeated. 'I really am.'

Phil swore violently. 'Look, Davey, you can grovel all you want, but the fact is I don't like you, and I never will.'

'You tell him, Phil!'

The unexpected voice made me jump, then I felt sick.

I turned to see two of Phil's most obnoxious friends, perhaps I should say followers, standing just behind me. I cringed at the thought of what they might have heard.

'Get lost, Johnson,' they said. 'Take your grovelling somewhere else.'

I left with the sound of their laughter in my ears.

'Wait until we tell the others about that creep' were the last words I heard.

Friday 16 March, 7.00 pm

Sure enough, Phil's friends spread the word that I had gone begging for forgiveness. To hear them tell it, you would think I had been down on my hands and knees, licking the mud off his shoes with my tongue, all the while crying my eyes out with shame and fear of what he would do to me. Still, it was bliss to go to swimming practices and not have to worry about him. Without the injection of his hatred and venom my fellow swimmers at least treated me like a human being – even while they laughed at the exaggerated story of my apology.

As Charlie had said, nobody (other than Phil, that is) really blamed me for what had happened at the last gala. They were disappointed, but knew that it could have happened to anyone. Probably they were just relieved that it had happened to me and not to them.

As Mr Bishop put it in his pep-talk at the beginning of the practice: 'Nothing is lost. We will just have to work that little bit harder and swim that little bit better.'

As I dived in for my first set of lengths I was determined to do my bit, work hard and prove that I had a part to play in our campaign to win the Nationals.

Competition was hotting up for places now, and everyone who was in with a chance swam hard and fought for the coach's attention and praise. After each practice a sheet was posted on the school's sports notice board with times and rankings of every member of the team printed on it. Each morning this board became the meeting place for the swimming club as we checked our positions and discussed who would make the team. With Phil out of the running, or rather the swimming, I was consistently placed first among the breaststrokers. If he didn't recover I could be as confident as anyone of a place on the team. There was nothing to be done about that, though, and I simply concentrated on keeping my stroke right and putting in extra-strong spurts whenever the coach was looking my way.

After practice I made my way home on foot, still too sensitive to Phil's jokes to risk bumping into him while on a trip to McDonald's with Charlie. As I kicked a stone along the footpath, a car drove past me and then stopped. Like a replayed scene from one of my happiest dreams, the window wound down with a screech, and a familiar blonde head poked out.

'Can we give you a lift, Dave?'

On this occasion Sophie sat in front with her father, and I was alone in the back seat. I stared adoringly at the back of her head, noting that her hair looked darker than usual – wet from swimming. Sophie's father did most of the talking – he at least seemed to have forgiven me – and I began to think that the lift had been his idea.

Sophie remained silent throughout the journey, so it was a great surprise when, as her father stopped to let me out, she suddenly asked him to wait for her for a few minutes, as she wanted to talk to me alone.

'Mind your step. That kerb's a killer,' was her father's parting remark. I didn't appreciate his humorous reference to my previous clumsiness, but he was the sort of man it was hard not to like.

Sophie walked silently beside me until we were a little way down the road and out of sight of her father. Then she stopped and we stood facing each other. She seemed uncertain as to why she was there.

'Sophie, I'm sorry about the party,' I began. 'I really never meant to hurt you. It's just that . . .' I stopped as she pressed her finger to her lips.

'Shut up, Dave,' she said softly. 'Charlie's been arguing your case for weeks now. I don't need to hear more excuses from you. I just wanted you to know that I've heard about your apology to Phil, and whatever the rest of the school might say I think you were very brave. My dad would say it showed backbone.' She smiled at the slightly awkward expression. 'I suppose I wonder if I've misjudged you, and been a bit hard on you.' She paused for a long moment and it was so quiet that I could hear my heart pounding in my chest.

Finally she continued: 'I sometimes think that there's more to you than meets the eye, and that perhaps all the best bits are hidden away inside.'

'Sophie,' I burst out. 'I . . .'

She shook her head and raised her hand to silence me.

'I'll be seeing you, Dave,' she called over her shoulder as she walked back to the car.

Chapter Thirteen

Sunday 18 March, 5.55 pm

Charlie was not happy.

'Why didn't you tell me! They're going to think I'm in fancy dress. I look like an undertaker,' he moaned.

Charlie's image was sacred to him and he always strutted around like a male model. All the world was a catwalk for Charlie. But not tonight: tonight he was dressed in a badly fitting black suit – something his mother had bought him for a family funeral. To make matters worse, Charlie had grown since the funeral and a good inch-and-a-half of ankle was exposed between trouser and shoe. I was dressed as usual – in jeans, sweatshirt and trainers.

'When I told her we were going to church, my mother absolutely insisted I wear a suit,' continued Charlie. 'You know what she's like about religion. If you knew this church wasn't like that then why didn't you tell me? What if someone spots us?'

'Can you imagine bumping into any of your friends in a church?' I asked Charlie, hoping to calm him down.

He shook his head and looked momentarily relieved.

'I should never have let you talk me into this,' he said in a more relaxed voice. 'I only agreed to come because it's my first opportunity to meet your brother. You've been keeping him under wraps for so long now that I was beginning to wonder if he was just a figment of your imagination. I guess that's why I made that slip with your mother.'

It took a moment to sink in; I hadn't been listening very carefully to Charlie's prattlings because I was busy watching for Chris's car, but eventually the sentence did register – forcefully. Forgetting for an instant that we were standing on a busy street corner, I spun around to face Charlie, and grabbed him by the lapels of his suit jacket.

'You did what?' I spat out the question. 'You let slip to my mother about Chris?'

'Not exactly . . .' He looked embarrassed and worked his jacket out of my grasp, then stepped away to a safe distance. 'These days every time I call you're out! The last time I asked for you, your mum seemed confused and said that she thought you were with me. She sounded concerned and I wanted to reassure her. I told her not to worry – that you must be with your brother.' Charlie took a worried look at my face. 'Don't worry, Dave, she didn't believe me; just laughed, and said that it was absurd – you didn't have a brother.'

'And I suppose you put her straight and explained everything!' I was livid with Charlie.

'Of course not,' he said with a shamed expression. 'I'd remembered what you'd said about it being a secret by then. It doesn't really matter, does it?' he asked hopefully.

Chris chose that moment to draw up at the kerb beside us.

'Don't you dare tell Chris about this,' I said, as we prepared to climb into the car.

The introductions didn't take long, and soon Charlie was back into his stride, seeming to have forgotten about both the suit and his big mouth. In fact, Chris and Charlie got on blazingly well. Some people seem to spark off each other, and it wasn't long before the car was filled with laughter. Charlie's stream of old jokes and stupid observations only faltered when Chris asked him how he felt about going to church.

'I'm looking forward to it,' said Charlie politely. 'About as much as I look forward to double French,' he whispered to me.

'So you don't find church boring?' asked Chris.

That stumped Charlie. Should he treat Chris as he treated all other adults, and try and charm him with what he thought he wanted to hear, or should he treat him like a prospective friend, in which case he could tell him the truth? I knew Charlie so well that I could almost see this argument taking place inside his head.

'Be honest,' I encouraged him.

'I have had one or two less than stimulating experiences,' said Charlie. 'But perhaps I've been unlucky. I'm sure your church will be different.'

He had chosen the middle ground: a little bit of truth, a little bit of charm.

'I hope you're right,' said Chris. 'This actually isn't my

church; I go to one in the city, but I have friends who go here and whenever I've visited it's been excellent.'

There was silence in the car for a few minutes.

'I'm a Catholic,' Charlie announced, completely out of the blue. He even managed to make it sound as if it were a vital part of his life. 'Is it a Catholic church we're going to?'

'No,' said Chris. 'It's not.'

'Oh,' said Charlie, as if he were considering an important issue.

I grinned at Charlie playing the Catholic. I had a strong suspicion that he was long overdue at the confessional.

'I did consider changing my allegiance once,' said Charlie. I began to wonder if this unexpected speech was going to have a punchline. 'There was this church on the local news – they met in a pub! I asked my mum if we could go to mass there. Sadly she wasn't tempted. If they'd met in an Italian restaurant it would have been a different story. She'd have been there like a shot!'

'That's not a real church,' I declared with all the authority of two months of Christianity under my belt. I was shocked when Chris challenged me.

'Why not?'

'Well,' I stammered, 'it just isn't.'

'It could be,' countered Chris. 'A church is made up of people, not bricks.'

I wasn't prepared to give in that easily.

'If church is just about Christians meeting together, then how come there are so many different ones?' I asked.

Chris was busy reversing into a small space between two parked cars, so he didn't answer me immediately.

'Do you have any idea how many Christians there are in the world?' he asked eventually. Charlie and I shrugged and looked blank (it was an expression we had perfected at school). 'Around 1,700 million,' said Chris. 'If you wanted them to worship in unison, you would need to cram every stadium in the world with Christians and then connect them via satellite. Even then people would be too tightly packed together to be able to sing with much enthusiasm. Look, we should go in,' he continued. 'The service is about to begin and we can talk more afterwards. I tell you what, I'll buy you both something to eat.'

I flashed an 'I told you so' look at Charlie – I had told him about Chris's generosity.

Inside the church it was unexpectedly bright and warm. We were greeted at the door, not by a black-robed and stern-faced clergyman, but by a friendly young woman. I could tell that Charlie liked the look of her because while she was talking he kept pulling down on his trousers, trying to disguise the shortfall around his ankles. As Chris chatted and Charlie squirmed, I looked around. The building was full, with people sitting not on pews but on moulded plastic chairs like the ones we used at school. When Chris led us to three empty seats, comfortingly near the back, Charlie and I exchanged glances. We weren't quite sure what to expect.

There were a few announcements and a prayer, then a band struck up and led us, the congregation, in singing. The songs must have been hymns of some sort, but were unlike any religious songs I'd ever heard. The words were traditional Christian, but the music was loud and moving. Charlie turned to me and raised his eyebrows. He seemed impressed.

As I looked around I realised that, unlike other church experiences I had had, this congregation wasn't entirely composed of pensioners – there were a lot of young people too.

I noticed that Charlie had already started to flirt with a group of girls sitting to our right. At the moment he was limiting himself to smiles and eye contact, but I was worried that even in the middle of a church service he might try to take things further. Before he could start exchanging phone numbers I dug him in the ribs and indicated that he should be facing forward.

Intending to set a good example, I turned my attention to the band. I froze, eyes riveted on the backing singers. The middle one had blonde hair, and even on stage, moving in time to the music, she looked more like an athlete than a performer.

It couldn't be Sophie – not here!

I shut my eyes and rubbed them, but when I looked again the vision had not disappeared. Incredible.

Hidden and anonymous in the middle of the large crowd, I enjoyed the rest of the music. I joined in where I could, but mostly I watched Sophie. I was transfixed by her and shocked by the coincidence that had led to our both being here. Once again, it seemed, God had heard my prayers and was working things out. Charlie, still distracted by the girls on his right, had not yet noticed

Sophie, and I put off telling him, unwilling to share this moment with anyone.

The music stopped and I watched as Sophie skipped down the few steps and took a seat on the front row. I could just see the back of her bowed head as the leader stood and said a few prayers. After the prayers, they announced a time for socialising, and people stood to greet one another. Sophie rose and looked back at the body of people behind her. After scanning the room and waving to various friends, her eyes came to rest on Charlie and me. A look of shock and surprise crossed her features, and then, to my delight, her face lit up and she broke into a huge smile. She left her seat and headed straight for us.

Charlie was still oblivious to her presence when I stepped past him to intercept her.

'Where are you rushing off to?' he asked.

Only then did he catch sight of Sophie. She was moving towards us, but her progress was slow. It seemed that everyone wanted to say hello as she passed.

'Sophie? Here?' said Charlie, visibly shocked. 'Did you know she'd be here, Dave?'

'Not a clue,' I said. 'I only spotted her a few minutes ago myself. I had no idea. Not that I'm complaining,' I added.

'Who'd have thought it?' said Charlie. 'Sophie, you and I meeting in a church, of all places.'

Finally Sophie escaped the last well-wisher and approached us.

'What are you doing here?' she asked.

'It's a long, long story,' I replied.

'And that's the truth,' added Charlie, with emphasis.

Before we could continue, Chris politely disengaged himself from the attentions of two old ladies in the row behind and turned to join us.

'You two don't hang around, do you?' he smiled. 'Dave told me you were a "girl-magnet",' he said to Charlie.

Anyone else, anybody in the whole world, would have had the decency to blush at such a comment, but Charlie accepted it as his due and as a compliment.

'Thanks,' he said. 'But actually I can't take all the credit for this one. This is Sophie. She's a schoolfriend – of both of us.'

'Sophie?' questioned Chris, looking at me. 'Surely not the one who . . .' He ground to a halt as I glared at him. 'Well, it's great to meet you,' he started again. 'I'm Chris, Dave's brother.'

'Dave's brother?' said Sophie. 'But I didn't think you had a brother, Dave.'

'I didn't think he had one either,' said Charlie. 'And neither did Dave. Not until a few weeks ago.'

'As I said, it's a long story.' I prepared to explain.

'And not one we have time for now,' added Chris as the leader of the service began to call people back to their seats. 'Why don't you join us for a bite to eat after the service, Sophie? If you can put up with the company, that is.'

I daydreamed my way through most of the remainder of the service – standing when the congregation stood, bowing my head when they prayed. After the Bible readings, an older man stood to speak.

I jerked to attention once during his talk, when I heard the word 'swimming'.

'I love to swim,' he said, 'and I was a pretty fair front-crawler in the days of my youth. The reason I still swim is that it's such a good work-out for the whole body. When I get out of the pool I feel that every muscle from the top of my head to the soles of my feet has been exercised.'

I remembered the feeling of utter exhaustion that I felt after practices, and agreed with the speaker.

'My brain sends the instructions to the different muscles, and as they work in co-ordination this tired old man moves smoothly through the water. It's wonderful! As you all know, the church is likened to a body in the New Testament. Christ is our head – he sends the orders – and we, his people, are the muscles, the hands and the feet that do his work in the world. When I swim I need every muscle of my body – even the ones I can't see and can't name – and as a church we need every member God has given to us if we are going to do the work that he calls us to do. Every Christian has a unique part to play. Something that can be done by nobody else. Every one of you sitting out there is equally and infinitely valuable and important. Nobody should look down on anybody else.'

It wasn't long before I had lost the track again but those few sentences had been exactly what I needed to hear as I struggled to know whether I would be any good as a Christian.

After the service Sophie, Charlie, Chris and I piled into the car and headed off to look for food.

'Somewhere a long way from school,' said Charlie, in response to Chris's question about where we wanted to go. 'I couldn't bear to run into any more friends wearing this.'

We ended up in one of the burger restaurants that were springing up all over town. Charlie was enthusiastic.

'Excellent,' he said as we took our seats. 'I've always wanted to try this place, but I've never been able to find anyone stupid enough to pay for me.'

'Charlie!' said Sophie.

Sophie and I ganged up to take Charlie to task for insulting Chris. Secretly I was pleased. It was obvious Charlie had decided that Chris could be a friend.

As we ate, we turned to more serious topics of conversation. Sophie had to be brought up to speed.

'And that's why Dave had to miss your party!' exclaimed Charlie as I reached the part about Chris's message stating a time and place when I could meet him.

'In that case,' said Sophie, 'I think Dave can consider himself completely forgiven. I'd never have recovered from the guilt if I thought I was the reason Dave had missed out on meeting a long-lost brother.'

She made this statement looking directly at me and reinforced its message with a dazzling smile. I melted from the inside out, and I felt so weak that for a second I was scared that I might slide off my seat onto the floor.

'Brilliant,' said Charlie, sounding anything but pleased. 'I guess that means I'll be seeing a lot less of you two then. You certainly won't want me knocking around like some useless third wheel.'

I blushed, still doubting that Sophie could care about

me in that way, and feeling that Charlie was making a fool of me. Fortunately, Chris took one look at me and burst into laughter. That made me blush even more but at least it broke the tension.

When we returned to the subject of church, both Charlie and I commented on the friendly atmosphere.

'I knew we were among some peculiarly kind people,' I said, 'when I noted that nobody laughed when they caught sight of Charlie in his suit.'

'I did consider introducing Charlie's trousers to his shoes. It's quite obvious they've never met,' said Sophie, causing Chris to splutter on his drink. 'But seriously,' continued Sophie, 'I'm really glad you liked it because that church is a second family to me.'

'That's exactly what it felt like,' said Charlie, jabbing his finger towards Sophie to emphasise his words. 'I've been trying to put my finger on it, but that's exactly the right way to describe it. Totally different to school. At school everyone is in competition, willing to do anything to anybody just to get what they want. I hate it!'

I was shocked to hear that even Charlie found school like that. I had always assumed that for him popularity was assured, and not something he had to work at.

'Yes!' said Sophie. 'Exactly! After the tensions of school I love to be with my church friends. I can't imagine how I could ever survive as a Christian without the rest of the church to keep me going. Oh, I'm sorry to go on,' said Sophie, obviously a little embarrassed at getting so carried away.

It was only later, after we had dropped Sophie and

Charlie home, that I had the opportunity to raise the subject of our parents with Chris.

'Chris, we've got to do something about Mum and Dad,' I began.

'I know,' said Chris. 'But let's keep things quiet for a little longer. OK?'

'Maybe, but I have a feeling it won't be long before they put two and two together and guess that you've reappeared on the scene. Perhaps they already have.'

'Why? What's happened?' said Chris, sounding really anxious.

I explained about Charlie's conversation with my mother.

'That does put a different complexion on things,' said Chris quietly. He lowered his head and gently massaged his eyes with his fingers for a moment. 'It was probably only cowardice that was making us put it off in any case,' he said, looking up at last. 'This is probably for the best.' He sounded as if he were trying hard to convince himself.

'So, what are we going to do?' I asked.

'No idea,' said Chris.

'You could come home with me right now.' It was an offer made out of duty more than enthusiasm for the idea. 'We could lay it all out on the table and let them do their worst.'

'No offence, Dave, but you have no idea how badly they could react. They think I murdered their baby daughter, remember? If we just drop in on them in private, without warning, I really think they might freak out, start screaming at me, and to be honest I don't think I could handle that. No, we need some way to make it a bit more low key.'

'I have one idea,' I said. 'The National Schools Swimming Gala is at the end of next week. If I'm selected to swim I'll be given tickets for the finals. I will invite Mum and Dad and tell them I'm giving a third ticket to someone I very much want them to meet. That way you'll encounter them in a noisy public place, which should take some of the pressure off, and Mum and Dad are far too image-conscious to throw a screaming fit in front of hundreds of people. They'd have no choice but to talk to you in a civilised manner. If everything goes well, I'll meet the three of you later, after the gala.'

'I note the way you've arranged to be safely somewhere else when the meeting actually takes place and the fireworks start,' said Chris.

'I have to admit that is the particular attraction of this plan,' I grinned. 'But I'm open to other suggestions, if you have any.'

'Not right now,' said Chris. 'But you'll be the first to know if I come up with anything better. In the meantime you must let me know if you make the team. When will it be decided?'

'We've got two more practices, Monday and Wednesday, to "state the case for our inclusion" as the coach puts it. The team will be posted on the sports notice board on Friday morning, leaving one week to prepare for the gala.'

Chapter Fourteen

Friday 23 March, 8.40 am

On Friday morning, the students walking the crowded school corridors were unusually subdued, quiet with expectation. It was well known that today was the day the team would be announced. Charlie and I were silent as together, and in step, we turned the last corner and walked up to a number of other swimmers clustered around the sports notice board.

As expected we found a single white sheet of paper pinned in the middle of the green felt board. It was not a team list, just a simple two-line note: 'All swimmers are requested to attend a meeting with Mr Bishop in Room 211 during the 11 am break this morning.'

'That's too cruel,' said Charlie. 'Trust the coach to be a sadist and string out the pain for as long as possible.'

'It's all right for you,' I said. 'It's not as if there's any doubt about your place. I, on the other hand, am very likely to be watching events from the stands, especially since Phil's been back and training this last week. I can't see the coach dropping him, and I can't see how there's room for us both on the team.'

'Stop worrying,' said Charlie. 'You'll be in. I promise.'

At break time the swimming club members filed silently into Room 211. The atmosphere practically crackled, charged with a volatile mixture of excitement and fear. I took a place next to Charlie and we settled down to await Mr Bishop's arrival. Sophie was sitting to our right and Charlie leant forward to flash her a 'fingers crossed' sign. Tension was obviously contagious if even people like Charlie and Sophie, for whom a place on the team was a foregone conclusion, looked stressed.

In the midst of all this nervous energy sat two people who looked positively bored: Phil and Sunita. For Sunita boredom was a habit. She was one of those people who seemed to be watching her own life play out from somewhere way back in the audience. She had told Sophie that she wasn't sure if she wanted to be selected, as it would mean missing a good film on TV that Saturday night! Phil was a different matter. There was no doubt about his determination and desire to be on the team. He was always a cool customer, but I couldn't help taking his apparent confidence as a bad sign. 'He must already have spoken to the coach and been assured of his place,' I thought.

Eventually Mr Bishop arrived, carrying an official-looking folder. He closed the classroom door behind him, walked to the teacher's desk, and, in the manner of sports teachers everywhere, perched on the corner of it.

'I'm sorry to prolong the agony,' he began. 'But I've

had some hard decisions to make. It's a harsh fact of life that there isn't room on the team for all of you, and therefore some of you are going to be disappointed. I didn't think it was fair for you to find out from a team sheet. Instead I wanted to take this time to personally congratulate every one of you. It's been a brilliant term for the swimming club, and there is not one person here who hasn't improved immensely and proved themselves very fine swimmers.'

'Oh, just get on with it, will you!' said Charlie, quietly enough to avoid any danger of being overheard by the coach.

'I am going to start,' said the coach, 'by announcing the junior age group team.'

For the next few minutes Mr Bishop's voice droned on through a list of events and the names of those who would be competing in them. Each name was greeted by a sigh of relief or a scream of delight, depending on the owner's personality. When the coach reached the end of his list I sympathised with those whose names had not been called – especially as I expected to be feeling the same emotions in just a few minutes' time. Most sat still with a blank look on their faces, but there were one or two brave smiles and, among the youngest, one or two tears escaped and slid down cheeks that were white with disappointment.

It was too much to expect the junior team's excitement to die down instantly, and as the coach picked up another sheet of paper there was still a lot of noise.

'Before I announce the senior team,' said the coach, 'I

want to explain that my task has been made that much more difficult by the rapid recovery of Philip Squire from his knee injury. As you all know, Dave Johnson, a newcomer to the club this term, has been swimming exceptionally well. If Phil were unavailable, then it would be a simple matter to pen Dave in as our senior breaststroker.'

My heart sank. 'Here it comes,' I thought. 'The verdict: "FAILED. So sorry you didn't make it onto the team. Better luck next time, LOSER."' I was so disappointed that I almost missed the coach's next words.

'And in fact, that is what I have decided to do. Dave will be the senior breaststroker. I have already spoken to Phil, and he understands that the team will be best served if he transfers to butterfly – another stroke at which he is more than proficient. With that little problem resolved, here is the rest of the team . . .'

I was elated. I was in. I hadn't failed. The coach had selected me! And it was no wonder Phil had looked bored. He had known what was coming and presumably he was less than thrilled about it. The rest of the team contained no surprises. Charlie was in, so was Sophie, and Sunita would have to set the video to catch Saturday night's film.

After Mr Bishop left, the room erupted. Everyone was speaking at once: some congratulating, some commiserating, some boasting about the records they were going to set at the gala. Sophie came over to join Charlie and me.

'We're all in!' she shouted excitedly. 'It's going to be brilliant. Just imagine a whole weekend of swimming together. We'll be at the best pool in the country and there'll be hundreds of people watching. Even the newspapers will be there to report the results.'

'Oh stop, please,' I said. 'You're making me feel ill! I've only just found out I'm on the team. Let me enjoy the feeling for a few moments at least.'

I phoned my news through to Chris that night. He tried to sound pleased for me but I could tell he had been hoping I wouldn't make it. It wasn't that he didn't care about me, but he dreaded the thought of a meeting with Mum and Dad.

'I suppose you've got a busy week then,' he said.

'Yes,' I replied. 'Swimming practices every night, Monday to Thursday, to practise starts and relay changes and things like that. Then on Friday morning we drive north to where the gala's being held. Heats will take place on Friday afternoon and Saturday morning, before the finals on Saturday night. By that time, if everything goes according to plan, we'll be well on our way to reuniting our family.'

'I hope so,' said Chris, without enthusiasm.

Monday 26 March, 8.50 am

'Where were you two last night?' said Sophie when Charlie and I walked into the class for registration on Monday morning.

'What's up?' said Charlie. 'We hadn't made any plans, had we?'

'I mean church,' said Sophie. 'Why weren't you there?'

Charlie looked mildly surprised, and my expression probably mirrored his.

'We didn't really think about it,' I said. 'Chris was busy this weekend and, well, we weren't invited or anything. We just didn't think about going back.'

'You don't need invitations, you know,' said Sophie. 'Although, if it helps, I'll happily write you one. You should have come. I was hoping I would see you there.'

'I'd love to have been there,' I said. 'But honestly, it just didn't cross my mind.'

'No problem,' said Sophie. 'Some of my church friends are meeting up on Wednesday. We could join them after swimming practice if you want.'

'Church during the week?' said Charlie. 'Not for me, I'm afraid, but Dave's the religious one. I'm sure he'll be up for it.'

As far as I was concerned, opportunities to spend more time with Sophie were not to be sniffed at.

'I'd love to come,' I said.

After Sophie had left, Charlie sat me down for one of his 'man to man chats', as he called them.

'David,' he addressed me formally, 'I will allow you to go to that strange religious gathering on one condition . . .' He paused for dramatic effect. 'The condition is that on Wednesday night you finally do yourself a favour and ask Sophie out. If you don't take your chance it'll be the end of term and you'll have all the Easter holidays to regret it.'

'Charlie, I couldn't,' I replied, going cold at the thought of taking such a risk. 'I'm sure she doesn't like me like that. What could Sophie see in me?'

'A question I have asked myself many times,' said Charlie, shrugging. 'But my quite considerable experience with women leads me to believe that she sees something that is hidden from the rest of us. You had better take your chance while it's there or I'll disown you.'

I promised to do my best.

Wednesday 28 March, 8.50 pm

Walking with Sophie through Southerton's dark deserted streets was exhilarating. Swimming practice was over and we were on our way to meet her friends. Sophie was in a wonderful mood. On the one hand she was excited, full of enthusiasm and dreams for the gala, which was only two days away, but she was also more relaxed in my company than I had ever known her to be. It seemed to me that her defences had been lowered and I had been given access to the real Sophie who lived inside. I felt almost drunk with the pleasure of being alone with her.

The walk came to an end, disappointingly quickly, outside a large and comfortable-looking house.

'Well, here we are,' said Sophie. It might have been wishful thinking, but I thought I detected a slight sense of disappointment in her too.

'And where is "here" exactly?' I asked.

'This is Ben's house, or his parents' to be more accurate.

Ben's one of my church friends; we use his house as a place to get together.'

She reached up to press the button of an old-fashioned door bell. Less than 30 seconds later, the door was thrown open by a boy of about our age.

'Sophie! What time do you call this?' he demanded, grinning and running a hand through his wildly tousled hair.

'Sorry, Ben, swimming practice ran over and then Dave and I had to walk all the way through town and up the hill from the old pool.'

'I guess you must be Dave then,' said the boy, extending his hand to me. 'I'm Ben. There are still a few people here,' he continued, as he led us through the house and back to a large kitchen.

'Hey guys,' he called as he entered. 'Sophie's finally here, and she's brought a friend called Dave.'

The group of ten or more people who were scattered through the kitchen, sitting on stools or counter tops or just leaning up against the cupboards, called out greetings and a few sarcastic remarks about the time of our arrival. Sophie wandered around the kitchen hugging and chatting to friends and making a fuss of the big black labrador.

Ben turned back to me.

'Are you another swimming fanatic like Sophie?'

'I'm not quite as much of a fanatic as Sophie, but I do swim,' I replied.

'Hungry after your practice?' asked Ben. 'Fancy some toast?'

Before I could decide if it would be impolite to accept his offer Sophie, who had obviously been eavesdropping on our conversation, called out an enthusiastic 'Yes please, Ben!' Someone else expressed an interest, and then the next person followed suit, until it became clear that Ben's toaster was going to be overworked for a while.

Twenty minutes later, as we sat around finishing off the last slices of toast, Sophie asked what had been discussed in the earlier part of the evening.

'We were looking at Romans chapter 12,' said Ben. 'It's the chapter that talks about not living like the "people of the world" but being changed by God into a new way of living. We each talked about what it was that we found hardest about living as a Christian at school or wherever.'

'Ben's problem is that he insists on snogging a different girl at every party he goes to,' called out one of the girls from the far side of the kitchen.

'I keep telling you – it's hard to resist when they throw themselves at me,' laughed Ben.

A damp tea towel came flying across the room, accompanied by an exasperated sigh: 'You are soooo . . . arrogant!'

'Easy!' said Ben laughing. 'I was only trying to re-heat the discussion. Anyhow, the only regular member we've not heard from tonight is Sophie. So over to you, Sophie: What is it you find hardest about living as a Christian?' He lifted the butter knife that he still held in his hand up to Sophie's mouth as if it were a microphone.

It seemed to me that Sophie took the question more

seriously than it had been intended. She was silent for a few moments before she spoke.

'It's funny you should ask that question tonight,' she said to Ben. 'I've been thinking a lot about that sort of thing lately. I think I've been very bad at living out my faith, particularly at school. Dave will tell you that most of the people at Southerton don't even know I'm a Christian.'

Sophie's speech felt like a confession and I desperately wanted to stick up for her, but it was true: I'd studied Sophie for years and it had never crossed my mind that she might be a Christian.

'It's not that I've done anything really wrong,' she continued. 'I've avoided most of the serious drinking and the drugs, and I don't seem to have Ben's problem with members of the opposite sex throwing themselves at me. It's the things I haven't done that I feel guilty about. I've been a sort of chameleon Christian – I've lived as a Christian at church and with you,' she said looking at her friends around the kitchen, 'but at school I've just blended in with everybody else. There's been nothing distinctive about my behaviour, nothing to show that I'm in any way different. I've known for a long time that that's wrong, but now I've decided that it's all going to change. I've already made my promises to God and now I'm telling you so that you can help to hold me to them.'

I think that everyone in the kitchen was moved by Sophie's honesty. They soon gathered around and promised to support her in her new commitment. I began to understand why Sophie valued the company of this group so much. There was a deeper level of friendship here than anything to be found among the gangs and cliques of school.

Her honesty also had the effect of helping other members of the group to be more open. People who admitted to having given only superficial answers during the discussion earlier in the evening now talked about the things that really bothered them. We discussed the difficulties of not getting drawn into gossiping when everybody was busy talking about someone's private life and problems. One of the boys in the group, who was a couple of years older than me, talked about the difficulty he was having working out how his career ambitions fitted in with God's plan for his life.

Ben admitted that he found it really hard to put other people first. 'I'm selfish, and I don't just mean with friends and family,' he said. 'I think a lot about people around the world. Some of them are starving and all I worry about is how to persuade Mum and Dad to buy me a new stereo or a better skateboard.'

I began to see more than I ever had before how Christianity affected every area of life. I was impressed by Sophie's commitment and I decided that I would have to do some serious thinking myself. Were there things about my life that I needed to consider changing?

Soon it was time to leave. I was walking home and Sophie, who would be picked up later, offered to see me to the door. Soon we were standing alone in the hallway. As ever I was overawed by her presence. She was too perfect. To extend our time together I asked the question that had been troubling me.

'Sophie, do you ever feel that living as a Christian is too hard? Do you ever wonder if it's worth it?' I was thinking in particular of the ridicule I had faced after 'doing the right thing' and apologising to Phil. Sophie paused to consider my question.

'Yes,' she admitted. 'I suppose that's why I've opted out for so long and just tried to take the easy route. But I don't for a second doubt that being a Christian is worth it.'

I nodded in agreement. I only had to look back over the past couple of months to see the change for the better that God had made in my life. I knew the effect of the cross: forgiveness and a relationship with God. All this had given me new purpose and a new sense of being important. I wasn't just an average student at Southerton Comprehensive; not just a vague inconvenience to my busy mother and father. I was loved by the God of all the universe!

Sophie opened the front door and walked with me out into the garden.

'It can be strange to think that God knows us better than we know ourselves, all the good and all the bad,' she said as we walked up the path to the front gate. 'And it's weird to think he cares about how we act, isn't it? How we treat our friends, what we do with our lives. He really cares . . .'

Sophie's voice faded out and she looked so beautiful in the light of the street lamps that I stood watching her, hoping against hope that she might be included in God's plans for my future. Fortunately she was too lost in her own thoughts to realise that I was staring at her rather more intently than would be considered polite. Eventually she spoke again.

'Thank you for coming, Dave,' she said. 'It's so wonderful to know there's another Christian in my class at school.'

Jolted from my reverie, I felt stung by the casual tone of her words and I wondered if that was all I was to her – just another Christian like Ben and the rest. On the other hand, perhaps Charlie was right. I was confused. Did I mean more to her than that? Might she consider going out with me? There was only one way to find out. With Charlie's encouragement, and his threats, ringing in my ears, I opened my mouth to ask the fateful question.

Chapter Fifteen

Friday 30 March, 10.50 am

I peered out through the coach window. The view was distorted by lashing rain that sent huge droplets of water streaming down the glass like marbles. 'At least they'll have enough water to fill the pool,' commented Charlie, who was sitting beside me.

We had just arrived at the National Swimming Centre – a huge, ultra-modern structure. It seemed a million miles from the decrepit old pool in Southerton.

'You almost expect the people walking in and out to be wearing space-suits,' said Charlie, who I think was as over-awed by the place as I was. 'Still, when it comes down to it, it's just a matter of moving through 50 metres of water as fast as you can. That's the thing to remember,' he said, as much to himself as to me.

The car park was already filling up with coaches and other vehicles as ours pulled into an empty space. Each of these was spilling its cargo of excited swimmers out onto the tarmac, where they huddled together under umbrellas to keep out of the pouring rain.

'All right,' called Mr Bishop, standing up and turning to speak to us from his seat at the front. 'Here's what we are going to do.' He went on to explain the procedure for registering and for finding our accommodation. 'Once you've settled in and made yourselves comfortable, be ready to meet at the main pool at 11.45. We're scheduled for a practice at midday before the heats this afternoon.'

Sophie joined Charlie and me in the registration line.

'Isn't this incredible? It's like the Olympics or some-thing. I feel so important.'

'I just feel nervous,' I replied.

'Oh Dave, you'll do brilliantly,' said Sophie, just before she was called forward. I watched her walk up to one of the officious-looking ladies who sat behind computers and entered competitors' names and details onto the database.

'Oh Dave, you'll do brilliantly,' mimicked Charlie. 'Hey, that reminds me. I'm supposed to have disowned you because you chickened out once again. Another fine opportunity to ask Sophie out wasted because of your cowardice. Honestly, I despair of you. I can't believe you've been my friend all these years and yet none of my style's rubbed off on you.'

'Charlie, I explained! I was going to ask her. We were alone and I actually had my mouth open to do the deed when her dad arrived to pick her up. Face it – there was no way I could ask her out in front of her father.'

'Excuses, excuses,' said Charlie. 'Just get a move on, or else I might have to take things into my own hands.'

'Don't you dare!' I shouted at Charlie's back as he walked forward to register.

The rest of the day passed in a whirl. All the heats for individual events took place that afternoon and evening, and we seemed to spend all our time rushing around the complex: from our accommodation, where Charlie and I shared a room with two other team members, to the pool for a practice, then back to the cafeteria for a meal, before more trips to and from the pool to swim or to support friends in their races.

At 9.30 that evening all 27 of us crowded into Mr Bishop's room to assess the day's results and plan our strategy for tomorrow. Most of us were excited and pleased with our performances, but dotted around were the sad faces of those who had not qualified for the finals, and for whom the gala was already over.

I was hugely relieved not to be numbered among that group. I had finished a very respectable second in my heat, and so was assured a place in the breaststroke final. Sophie, Charlie and Phil had also qualified. Phil had experienced a few desperate moments as he had been placed third in his heat and so had been forced to wait to see if he qualified as one of the two fastest losers, which, in the end, he did.

'It's been a good day,' said Mr Bishop, after commiserating with those who had not qualified. 'We've got more than our fair share of swimmers through to the individual

finals, and if we swim well in tomorrow's heats for the team events, then we should qualify for the finals in all ten relays.'

'What can we do about St Jude's?' asked a team member from her cramped position on the floor. St Jude's was a Catholic school from up north, and every single one of their swimmers had qualified for the finals – all but two had won their heats outright.

'Nothing,' replied Mr Bishop. 'We do our best and hope our best is better than theirs.'

'We could steal their steroids,' said Charlie. 'I swear they're on them.'

'Enough!' said Mr Bishop. 'Off to bed, all of you, and get a good night's sleep. You'll need your energy tomorrow.'

On any other school trip those words would have led to a riot that would continue through the night, but not this time. This was serious, and everyone took the coach at his word and retired to rest. I told Charlie that I would meet him in the room in a few minutes. I had two phone calls to make.

The first was to my parents. Back in Southerton my mum answered the phone.

'You'd better get the car filled with petrol,' I began, still full of my success.

'You qualified then? Well done. I'm so very proud of you!' I heard her calling out the news to my father and she sounded genuinely pleased. Just as my mother was about to hang up, I prepared to drop my bombshell.

'Mum, there will be someone in the seat beside you tomorrow night that I very much want you to meet.'

'Who is that?' asked my mother, and her voice suddenly had a hard, cold edge.

'I'm not telling you,' I said, 'but it's really important you meet them.'

The conversation became difficult. Mum tried desperately to remember a business meeting she needed to be at, but I refused to let her off the hook. It was obvious that, because of Charlie's indiscretion, she at least suspected who it was I was so anxious for her to meet. I made her promise that they would be there, and in the end I hung up, shaking slightly with emotion, but at least confident they would come.

Then I called Chris.

'So, how did it go?' he asked, trying to pretend that he had nothing more on his mind than a brotherly concern for my swimming career.

'I'm in,' I replied simply.

'And?'

'And Mum and Dad are going to be there.'

'Good,' he said, without much conviction. 'I guess your plan's going ahead then.'

'Yep,' I replied. 'Just go to the seat numbered on your ticket and you should run into Mum and Dad. From then on it's up to you, and to them, I suppose.'

'I bet it'll be a bundle of laughs,' said Chris sarcastically. 'If everything goes to plan, we'll meet you in the car park afterwards. Right?'

'I hope so,' I said, meaning it from the bottom of my heart. 'I know you think I've taken the coward's way out by not being there when you meet, but I promise I will be praying for you.'

'I know,' said Chris. 'But that doesn't make it any easier

to actually go through with it. Still, you need your beauty sleep, so I'll let you go, and hopefully see you tomorrow – for a joyous reunion.'

He hung up, leaving me to consider how the worry about tomorrow's meeting was driving Chris, normally so laid back and full of trust in God, to sarcasm.

Saturday 31 March, 4.15 pm

By late Saturday afternoon I didn't know what to do with myself. I couldn't even worry properly, because I kept getting distracted from worrying about one thing by a wave of worry about something else! I was petrified about the gala. Already the huge spectator stands in the swimming area were filling up, and a capacity crowd was expected for the finals. I couldn't bear to think of what it would be like to make a stupid mistake in front of that many people. Then there were Chris and my parents to consider. Presumably they would soon be on their way and driving towards a meeting that would have a huge impact on all our lives.

Finally, there was Sophie. The situation with her was at least as important to me as any one of my other concerns. How did she feel about me? I still wasn't sure. Of course she was nice to me, but then she wouldn't willingly hurt a fly. Perhaps she just felt sorry for me.

I knew that I was going to have to do something. Charlie's threat about taking things into his own hands had not been entirely idle. He was quite capable of confronting Sophie and telling her how I felt. One thing I was

certain of: the only thing worse than being rejected by Sophie would be being rejected by Sophie second hand, through Charlie.

I sat and stewed while everything churned around and around in my mind. Eventually it was all too much for me. Jumping up from the table where I had been sitting drinking juice with Charlie and a few others, I rushed out of the dining hall and towards the cluster of public phones in the corridor. As fast as possible I dialled home. Perhaps I could still catch them and tell them not to come!

'The number you have dialled is busy,' announced the annoying recorded message. I slapped the plastic dome of the booth in frustration and slammed the phone hard back down into its cradle. Someone tapped me on the shoulder.

'Are you all right, Dave?' It was Mr Bishop, and I noticed Charlie hovering behind his left shoulder, an anxious look on his face. 'Are you feeling OK? You don't look too good.' Mr Bishop tried again. 'I don't want you swimming if you're ill.'

'I'm fine, honestly. Just trying to reach my family.'

Mr Bishop looked concerned for a moment, but was eventually persuaded to leave me in Charlie's care.

My worries were still on my mind that evening as I walked with Charlie across the complex, through the competitors' entrance and down to the men's changing room. But my best friend had at least managed to calm me down and talk me out of trying to call the whole thing off. I now

felt I could cope with the evening. We would change into our swimming kit and tracksuits, before going to take our places with our team on the lower level of grandstand seating that was reserved for swimmers and coaches.

'Well, here we go,' said Charlie, as we walked out of the changing room and onto the poolside.

Already, a quarter of an hour before the first of the junior races, the stands were almost full.

'Hold on a minute,' I said to Charlie. 'I'm just going to see if my parents have arrived.'

I walked over to an information station and looked at the layout plan to see where the seat numbers that I had memorised were located. They were in the second tier of seats, right above our team position. As I walked back to Charlie I scanned the rows for familiar faces.

'Any joy?' asked Charlie.

'They'll be sitting right above us,' I replied. 'But I don't think they're here yet, and in any case it will be impossible to see them from where we're sitting because they're on the next level up above us.'

'I'm sure it will all work out,' said Charlie, who now knew how much rested on tonight's meeting.

'I really hope so,' was the most confident reply I could muster.

When we reached the team area we found that Sophie had saved two seats for us. Charlie ostentatiously motioned for me to take the one next to Sophie. Seeing that I had no choice, I did so.

'How are you two feeling?' asked Sophie.

'Hanging on,' I replied grimly.

Soon the junior finals were under way. We screamed ourselves hoarse as our team mates swam, and clung white-knuckled to our seats as we waited for the team scores to be posted after each race.

By the time the junior relays were over we were placed third, a point behind the second-placed team and well to the rear of St Jude's.

Sophie, Charlie and I huddled together to consider our standing.

'We can still win it,' said Charlie, ever the optimist.

'Yeah, if St Jude's stop swimming now,' I replied.

'No, it is possible,' said Sophie. 'Team relays count for double points, and we've got a real chance in those – this term they've been our strongest events. All we have to do is try to stay in touch through the individual events and then give it to them in the relays.'

'That's the spirit,' said Charlie. 'Don't let Dave's pessimism get you down. He has no idea about assessing his chances – in anything.' He looked at me and I knew what chance he had in mind.

Charlie was the first out of the three of us to swim. Ten minutes before his race was called he made his way to the poolside. He was still cracking jokes and making out it was no big deal, but it was quite apparent how nervous he was.

When he took his place on the starting block the tension grew until it was almost unbearable. As the gun fired, Sophie and I jumped to our feet and started screaming encouragement.

Freestyle is really the blue-ribbon event, and as always Charlie was up against the very best swimmers at the gala.

He set out at a ferociously fast pace and as he dipped into a tumble turn at the far end of the pool he was swimming almost level with the leader. Sophie and I had to be careful not to leap right off the stand in our excitement as we cheered him on. Soon we realised that he was tiring too fast. Over the closing metres he lost touch with the leader and was overhauled by a second swimmer.

It was only when the race was over that I noticed that Sophie had grabbed hold of my hand and was still holding it. She dropped it in embarrassment and I looked away, managing to disguise my feelings by moving to congratulate Charlie, who was coming up the stairs towards us.

'Brilliant,' I called. 'Third place! It's a medal position.'

'I should have done better,' said Charlie, throwing his goggles down onto his seat in disgust. 'I let the excitement get to me and set out too fast, then died at the end. I'll show them what's what in the relays though,' he promised. 'I'll slaughter them over 50 metres.'

Sophie swam next and swam brilliantly, earning us second-place points and pulling us back a little closer to the leaders. The much-loved Sophie received a cheer from the team as she returned to her seat. She had achieved the best result of the evening so far.

A few minutes later Mr Bishop gathered us together.

'OK,' he said. 'We're hanging on, and we're still in with a chance. If we can just narrow the gap a little in the next two races we can give it all we've got in the relays. Phil, Dave – it's up to you. If you both place in the top three we can still do it.'

Phil and I walked down to the poolside, together but in silence. I started to warm up and after a minute Phil left me to register for his race.

'Phil,' I called, and then ran a few steps to catch him.

'Yeah?' he replied.

'I just wanted to wish you luck,' I said.

'Thanks.'

I watched Phil's race over my shoulder as I lined up with the other breaststroke competitors to register and be assigned a lane. It didn't go well for him. He simply wasn't as good at butterfly as he was at breaststroke. In the end he finished the race in seventh place and climbed from the pool looking dejected.

I resolved to swim the race of my life. I had to prove that I was worth my selection. I had completely forgotten about Chris and my parents, but as I stepped onto the block in lane three I was afforded a panoramic view of the entire arena. Automatically my eyes searched for my team mates and I caught sight of Charlie and Sophie already standing and waving their encouragement. Then I lifted my eyes and saw Chris and my parents.

Things didn't look good. The body language was appalling. All three were sitting still and in silence. Mum and Dad had their arms folded. The pained expression on Chris's face as he watched me made him look like a prisoner looking down on the outside world from the confines of his cell. For a second my brain whirled and I felt sick. Instinctively I cried out to God and was rewarded by a sudden feeling of peace. Clutching at that feeling, I ruthlessly thrust all thoughts of my family from my mind.

They were in God's hands now and I had other things to think about.

The starter called us to take our marks and I leant forward into my starting position, my whole body tensed. Time seemed to stop and for what seemed like hours I crouched there, exposed to the gaze of thousands of people. Surprisingly, I didn't feel nervous, just compressed and ready, like a charge about to explode. I reminded myself of Charlie's advice: 'Don't let the occasion get to you; take it slowly at first, save something for the last 25 metres.'

There was an explosion to my right and for a nanosecond I was confused. What had happened? Then impulse took over, and even before I consciously realised that the starter's gun had fired I was diving out over the still blue water.

The favourite, from St Jude's naturally, swam to my right and for the first length I concentrated on keeping tucked in close behind him. As we turned, I made my move. I gulped extra deeply for air, filling my lungs to bursting, and then I accelerated. I didn't know it was there myself, but from somewhere deep inside of me the adrenaline pulled up an extra gear.

I started to gain on the favourite and then there was clear water ahead of me. And then the wall.

I stretched forward with both hands, gave one last violent kick, and then touched – in first place!

I pulled myself up out of the water in time to see our section of the grandstand going wild. Charlie and Sophie were dancing, the coach was applauding, and the whole team were on their feet. Once again I lifted my eyes to my family. My mum was still in her seat but was applauding wildly with clapping hands held high above her head. Even more amazing, my father and Chris were on their feet with their arms around each other, cheering and cheering my success. I waved, and they waved back exuberantly, continuing to smile and cheer at the same time.

Even the joyful reception I was given by the team a few minutes later couldn't compete with that moment. My hope for my family rose to a new level.

For me, the relays that followed were an anticlimax. In spite of Charlie's optimism and the coach's planning, we really couldn't compete with St Jude's. They were simply in a class above us, and above all the other schools for that matter. We finished the night in second position.

To our surprise, Mr Bishop was ecstatic.

'I wouldn't have told you this beforehand,' he said to the assembled team, 'because it would have been terrible psychology, but the truth is that I never even dreamed we would do this well. I really only hoped that we wouldn't be embarrassed. You should be proud of yourselves. It is probably wrong of me to single out anyone by name, but I do think Dave, who only joined the club this term, deserves a special mention as our only first-placed swimmer.'

'Speech! Speech!' shouted Charlie.

To my utter horror everyone, including the coach, took him seriously and quietened down for me to say a few words. At a loss, I looked around at my team mates. Inspiration came from an unexpected quarter when I

caught sight of Phil, sitting alone and unhappy at the back of the group.

'I would like to say a few words of thanks,' I began in a surprisingly strong voice. 'I would like to thank Phil Squire, who selflessly, and for the good of the team, agreed to move to butterfly to make room for me to swim breast-stroke. I think he deserves at least as much credit as I do.'

The whole team turned to look for Phil, and as they clapped him I was rewarded by the bright smile on his face.

As we made our way back to the changing rooms, Phil walked up beside me.

'You're a good man, Davey,' he said. 'I hope that from now on we can be friends.'

'I think that might be possible,' I replied, returning his smile. 'If you would only stop calling me Davey!'

As I changed, I prepared myself mentally for the rendez-vous with Chris and my parents. Charlie slapped me on the back as I stood to leave the changing room.

'I'll be thinking of you,' he said. 'And I bet you have good news for me when we meet up later. You will be at the competitors' party, won't you?'

'Yeah, I'll be there,' I replied.

Feeling desperately alone, I strode out of the doors and into the huge car park, which by now was practically empty. Way out on the far side, I spotted Chris standing alone by the side of his beaten-up old car. The absence of my parents caused me to fear the worst, and I walked towards him, filled by a rapidly growing anxiety.

We both spoke at the same moment, suddenly calling out to each other as I stepped within earshot.

'Where are Mum and Dad?' I called anxiously.

'Dave, you were brilliant!' shouted Chris.

'But where are Mum and Dad?' I tried again.

'They've gone home.'

'Oh no,' I said. 'Things went badly?'

'No, not in the end,' said Chris. 'It was tense for a while. Your mum was the worst. She said hello, said she was glad I was well, but then refused to speak another word to me. She kept up a stony silence through the whole gala. Up until your win, that is! That shook even her out of her mood. It was a false spring though and a few minutes later she went back into her shell.'

'Chris, I'm sorry,' I said. 'It must have been horrible. I honestly thought that everything would be OK when they actually saw you. I guess you were right, and I misjudged how strongly they felt. How do you feel now?'

'I think I would feel absolutely terrible,' said Chris, 'if it wasn't for this.'

Out of his pocket he pulled a crumpled photo and handed it to me. It was on stiff card and had the almost unreal colours that were typical of old colour photographs. The subject of the picture was a young boy, riding a donkey along the beach. He was smiling and waving to the camera.

'Read the back,' suggested Chris. I turned the photo and found a date and a line of faded and smudged script.

It read simply: 'My beloved son on his birthday.' I looked at Chris, not quite understanding.

'Dad gave it to me just a few minutes before they left, while your mum was in the toilet. He said that he has carried this with him every day for the last 20 years. He said that he had never stopped thinking about me, wondering where I was and what I was doing. He said that he had searched and searched, but eventually given up, deciding that I didn't want to be found. He said that he would meet me anytime and anywhere I wanted, and that he would work on your mum until she came around and accepted me back into the family! It was incredible, Dave,' said Chris with tears in his eyes. 'I never imagined, not in my wildest dreams, that he would still love me. But he does – I could see it in his eyes!'

Chris left to drive home, thrilled with his memories of a meeting that, in the end, had gone better than he had thought possible. I was pleased for him and for my father, and the future of our family seemed brighter than it ever had before, certainly since the days when my sister had been alive.

As I walked into the party that had been laid on for competitors I was still absorbed by thoughts of my family. I looked around the crowded room, searching among the hundreds of people for a familiar face. Phil saw me and came towards me.

'Charlie's been looking for you, Dave. He and Sophie, and a couple of others, have headed back for one last look at the pool before we go. I told him I'd let you know where he was.'

I thanked him and walked out of the reception and back towards the pool area. Everything seemed to be locked up, and I was just about to return, defeated, when I noticed that one particular door was wedged open, just a crack, by a discarded flip-flop. That looked like Charlie's handiwork to me, and I slipped through the door. Once inside I could hear giggling and I headed towards the noise. At the poolside I found Charlie with Sophie and another girl.

'Dave,' called Charlie. 'Glad you could make it. We thought you might like one last chance to relive your famous victory before we return to Southerton and the horrors of GCSEs. This, by the way, is Amanda,' said Charlie pointing to the girl at his side. 'She is the champion freestyler from St Jude's. If you can't beat them, join them,' he whispered to me over his shoulder.

I looked at Sophie, who had taken off her shoes and was sitting at the pool's edge, dangling her feet into the water.

'Amanda and I are just leaving,' said Charlie, and in a flash I realised I had been set up. In seconds Sophie and I were alone at the poolside. All the external lights were out and only the underwater ones were on. Everything was bathed in a soft blue light that flickered and darted as Sophie's feet disturbed the water. She was staring down into the depths and seemed unlikely to speak anytime soon. I kicked off my socks and shoes, and sat down beside her, lowering my feet into the water.

'Charlie said that you wanted to speak to me about something personal and important,' said Sophie. 'Do you?'

'Yes,' I replied. 'I do. Trouble is, I'm not very good at "personal and important".'

'Try me,' said Sophie. 'It might be easier than you think.'

I took a deep breath.

'Sophie, I know this is probably stupid, so don't be offended, but would you, could you, ever . . . consider going out with me?' I finished in a rush.

Sophie smiled, and to my relief it was a smile of genuine warmth, and not one of amusement.

'Dave, I'd love to,' she replied. 'I've been hoping and waiting for you to ask me for the last few weeks.'

I tried to restrain myself – silly little dances of joy would not be appropriate at this moment. Then she brought me down to earth.

'I would love to,' she repeated, 'but I can't.' My excitement was over. I stared down into the water as she continued. 'You see, I decided long ago that I would only ever go out with a Christian.'

I sat in silence for a moment, devastated. I hadn't really heard anything she had said after that terrible 'can't'. I tried to be brave and generous.

'I understand,' I replied, forced to fake a cough to disguise the real reason for the huskiness of my voice.

To my surprise, Sophie burst out laughing.

'Dave, I was joking. You are a Christian!'

'Hey, that's right!' I jumped to my feet and pulled her up with me. 'At the beginning of this term I wasn't, but now I am. What incredible timing!'

'The sky's the limit for us now,' whispered Sophie later,

as we stood close together in the blueness. 'We're together and you've found the answers to some of the most important questions of life.'

THE END

Recommended further reading

Why Jesus?
Questions of Life
Searching Issues
30 Days
The God Who Changes Lives, Vols 1, 2 & 3

These can be ordered by calling the Alpha Resources Hotline on 0845 7581 278.

If you are interested in finding out more about the Alpha course or in attending a course near you, details can be found on the Alpha course website (alphacourse.org) or by contacting the Alpha Office, Holy Trinity Brompton on 020 7581 8255

the shock of your life

by Adrian Holloway

Dan, Becky and Emma have
one thing in common.
They just died. Were
they ready?

Buy the book and
visit the web site.

www.theshockofyourlife.com

ADRIAN HOLLOWAY was a newspaper football and
feature writer for *The Times*. He then worked for the
BBC as a TV sports presenter, and has now given up
his career to work full time as an evangelist for New
Frontiers International in the Midlands.

 Kingsway Publications

Alpha

This book is an Alpha resource. The Alpha course is a practical introduction to the Christian faith initiated by Holy Trinity Brompton in London, and now being run by thousands of churches throughout the UK as well as overseas.

For more information on Alpha, and details of tapes, videos and training manuals, contact the Alpha office, Holy Trinity Brompton on 0207 581 8255, (home page: http://www.alpha.org.uk), or STL, PO Box 300, Kingstown Broadway, Carlisle, Cumbria CA3 0QS.

Alpha Hotline for telephone orders:
0845 7581 278 (all calls at local rate)

To order from overseas:
Tel +44 1228 512512
Fax +44 1228 514949

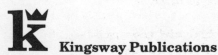 **Kingsway Publications**

 Alpha

Alpha titles available

A booklet – given to all participants at the start of [Alp]ha course. 'The clearest, best illustrated and most chal-[lenging] short presentation of Jesus that I know.' – Michael Green

[Why Ch]ristmas? The Christmas version of *Why Jesus?*

[Qu]estions of Life The Alpha course in book form. In fifteen compelling chapters Nicky Gumbel points the way to an authentic Christianity which is exciting and relevant to today's world.

Searching Issues The seven issues most often raised by participants on the Alpha course: suffering, other religions, sex before marriage, the New Age, homosexuality, science and Christianity, and the Trinity.

A Life Worth Living What happens after Alpha? Based on the book of Philippians, this is an invaluable next step for those who have just completed the Alpha course, and for anyone eager to put their faith on a firm biblical footing.

Telling Others: The Alpha Initiative The theological principles and the practical details of how courses are run. Each alternate chapter consists of a testimony of someone whose life has been changed by God through an Alpha course.

Challenging Lifestyle Studies in the Sermon on the Mount showing how Jesus' teaching flies in the face of modern lifestyle and presents us with a radical alternative.

30 Days Nicky Gumbel selects thirty passages from the Old and New Testament which can be read over thirty days. It is designed for those on an Alpha course and others who are interested in beginning to explore the Bible.

The Heart of Revival Ten Bible studies based on the books of Isaiah, drawing out important truths for today by interpreting some of the teaching of the Old Testament prophet Isaiah. The book seeks to understand what revival might mean and how we can prepare to be part of it.

All titles are by Nicky Gumbel, who is on the staff of
Holy Trinity Brompton

——— ❖ ———